"I consider
quickly, go

"A close friend.

The secret she held made her uncomfortable as she delivered the last, but...she had texted him. Asked him to call. He'd declined.

She'd figured he was breaking up with her.

Had even considered that maybe she'd wanted him to do so...

And started to get a bit miffed. He was the one who'd said he needed to talk. Why was she the only one doing so?

"What about you? How do you view us?"

He seemed to give the matter real thought. Continued to study her, as she was assessing him. Eye to eye. Just as they'd always done.

"Much like you do," he finally said.

So she'd gotten the answer right?

Where did that lead them? Where was he going with this?

Should she tell him about the embryo? The procedure? Tell him what was going on?

With him sitting there, meeting her gaze so openly, she wanted to. Badly.

He wasn't just a friend. In some ways he was her best friend. The one she trusted to have her back more than any other.

One whose back she'd die to protect.

She needed to tell him.

Dear Reader,

Happy holiday season!

Have you ever, just for an hour or two, stepped outside the rules you've given yourself to live by and just let your heart fly? Sometimes the heart knows what the heart needs. And sometimes an hour of giving in to temptation changes your whole life. If you're lucky, the two come together to give you something you didn't know you needed.

Sometimes a book shows you something you needed to see. I wrote Olivia's story a couple of years ago, and many books later, I can still remember scenes vividly. I see her driving down the highway, I feel her emotions and I can hear her thoughts. Olivia has a great life. She's content. She has happy moments, great friends, a career she loves. She's where she wants to be. And then she makes one reckless choice and it all comes tumbling down around her.

Olivia taught me that while it's great to have a plan, and be disciplined and take control of your life, it's also imperative that you listen to your heart. We aren't meant to live by our minds alone. True happiness comes when heart and mind live together. I hope the magic of the holidays finds you this season and that your heart speaks up!

Tara Taylor Quinn

Her Christmas Future

TARA TAYLOR QUINN

HARLEQUIN
SPECIAL
EDITION

HARLEQUIN®

SPECIAL
EDITION™

Recycling programs
for this product may
not exist in your area.

ISBN-13: 978-1-335-40811-2

Her Christmas Future

Copyright © 2021 by TTQ Books LLC

This edition published by arrangement with Harlequin Books S.A.

For questions and comments about the quality of this book,
please contact us at CustomerService@Harlequin.com.

Harlequin Enterprises ULC
22 Adelaide St. West, 40th Floor
Toronto, Ontario M5H 4E3, Canada
www.Harlequin.com

Printed in U.S.A.

Having written over ninety novels, **Tara Taylor Quinn** is a *USA TODAY* bestselling author with more than seven million copies sold. She is known for delivering intense, emotional fiction. Tara is a past president of Romance Writers of America and a seven-time RITA® Award finalist. She has also appeared on TV across the country, including *CBS Sunday Morning*. She supports the National Domestic Violence Hotline. If you need help, please contact 1-800-799-7233.

Books by Tara Taylor Quinn

Harlequin Special Edition

The Parent Portal

Having the Soldier's Baby
A Baby Affair
Her Motherhood Wish
A Mother's Secrets
The Child Who Changed Them
Their Second-Chance Baby
Her Christmas Future

The Daycare Chronicles

Her Lost and Found Baby
An Unexpected Christmas Baby
The Baby Arrangement

The Fortunes of Texas

Fortune's Christmas Baby

Visit the Author Profile page
at Harlequin.com for more titles.

For the generations of Cookie Day bakers whose hearts are forever joined—Mimi, Mima, Rachel and Morgan—our love is my mainstay and you are my gifts.

Chapter One

How could she have been so stupid? She was a *doctor*!

She *knew* what was at stake.

How could she have thought, even for a second, that she was allowed a few minutes of letting go, of breaking down?

She could forgive herself the overindulgence of wine.

But what had come after...

There was no excuse.

She had to get to Christine.

On the drive back to Marie Cove from her ex-husband's luxury penthouse apartment just outside of Los Angeles, Dr. Olivia Wainwright couldn't stop castigating herself.

As the sun rose from the horizon, turning night into day, her panic rose right along with it.

She was overreacting. She knew it. She also knew that the risk she'd taken was real. That the timing made it so.

Her volunteer shift at the women's center was due to start in just hours. She had to get home. Showered.

And get her hands on a levonorgestrel pill. Even the thought of the Plan B morning-after contraceptive made her cringe. Not so much because of the hormonal interruption in her system, but because if an egg had been in her fallopian tube she could already be getting pregnant. And a pill would effectively bring an end to that.

Thinking of Lily, and so many of her tiny, suffering patients in the neonatal unit where she worked, she knew it had to happen that way.

And cursed herself for even allowing the possibility.

Even as she ran through a mental list of possibilities for procuring the pill. Any number of her colleagues would provide one for her. Her own gynecologist would.

The thought of any of them knowing how incredibly irresponsible she'd been had her close to tears.

Only her gynecologist knew about Lily.

Her gynecologist…and Christine.

Owner and founder of the Parent Portal, a well-known private fertility clinic, Christine was also Olivia's closest friend.

Her friend's happiness, her marriage and, mostly, the pending birth of Christine's second child were all miracles that Olivia celebrated wholeheartedly.

Just as Christine had turned to Olivia when Christine had been asked to be a surrogate for a frozen embryo the year before, Olivia now needed Christine.

Things had seemed a little hectic back then, but they'd all worked out better than anyone could have imagined.

It was always darkest before the dawn.

Situations weren't always as bad as they seemed.

The empty platitudes were irritating her beyond her ability to cope, so Olivia pushed the button on her steering wheel, asked the automated system to call Christine Elliott-Howe and waited for her friend to pick up.

Scents of Olivia wafted through the air. Her perfume. Her sex.

Wandering around in black boxer briefs, sipping from his second cup of the dark roast Colombian coffee he'd brewed for his ex-wife—and she'd declined—Martin Wainwright looked out past the city skyline to the ocean just beyond. Filling his gaze with magnificent views that didn't include her waist-length dark hair, creamy tanned skin and chocolaty eyes that always made him feel like he was melting. In another hour he'd be out having his day, playing in a charity golf tournament and then on to the spa, after which, in his newly cleaned black tux without the satin trim, he'd be attending a five-hundred-head-count private birthday party for someone he barely knew.

His parents, from their perch in heaven, wouldn't understand that one. Why go to a party for a man who wasn't your friend? A man you weren't sure you even liked or trusted?

Though they'd died years apart, his parents were back together in his thoughts. The fact they'd come to mind at that moment didn't surprise him overly much. They'd been a poor, overlooked and seemingly unsuccessful pair, but their great love had been his personal life guide forever. Their commitment was a pinnacle he was never going to reach.

He'd be reaching a whole new class within the next few days, though. His flight on the private jet Sunday morning would give him ample time to write the speech he'd give to a graduating class of IT specialists in Rome—and the stipend he was being paid to do so would make his parents proud.

They'd raised a scale-mountains type of guy, teaching him that there were no limits to possibilities if he invested himself fully in whatever endeavor he took on. Every success he had was another win for them. His bare feet sinking into carpet so plush it could be someone's pillow, he allowed himself another second or two to reflect, maybe to wallow in his lover's abrupt departure, before taking his cup with him into the bathroom. The three-head, walk-in tiled shower had seemed like major overkill when he'd bought the place, but he'd grown to appreciate the overall massage they provided his forty-one-year-old muscles every morning.

Pushing thoughts of Olivia as far back in his consciousness as he could shelve them, knowing from years of experience that not thinking about her so much was the only way he'd be able to keep his ex-wife in his life, he stood under the tri-stream spray and focused on the work ahead of him that day. On the men he'd be with on the golf course, the two who'd invited him to enjoy an hour of benefit at their spa and the three groups he'd be talking to at the party later that evening. In all three cases, at all three functions, he had one goal. Not to enjoy himself, but to part the men with their charitable donations.

If all went well, and he had every reason to believe it would, he was set to raise half a million dollars by night's end. And Fishnet could help hundreds more underprivileged kids successfully climb to the top of their own chosen mountains.

No amount of achieved success, effort or money was going to make this right.

Still in the previous evening's formfitting black dress and three-inch black wedges, Olivia walked into the Parent Portal's back door just behind Christine.

"You really didn't have to haul yourself in here so early on a Saturday morning," she said for the third time. Christine had insisted on meeting her as soon as Olivia hit town.

"You're my friend," was the reply. Each time.

"How are you feeling?" Olivia asked while she

faced up to the incredibly stupid thing she'd done. She focused on Christine's bump, her impending motherhood, because she'd failed to deal with her jealousy over Christine's first pregnancy.

Because she'd never dealt with the pangs raised when Christine had given birth the year before.

William Ryder Howe was one of the most loved babies ever.

His aunt Olivia adored and spoiled him; she'd had the important distinction of being the first one, other than Christine, to feel him kick.

"At the moment I'm feeling worried about you," Christine said, turning on the light in her private office as they entered. She offered to make tea and then set about doing so without waiting for Olivia's response.

A neonatologist of some renown, Olivia took her leftover-dressed-up self to the couch and sat down on the edge of one cushion, legs together, hands in her lap. If only she'd managed to maintain such decorum the night before.

Damn Martin and the fire he'd always been able to light within her. What was wrong with her? Even after what turned out to be an unsuccessful marriage, she couldn't seem to get him out of her system.

Which was no excuse for her current situation. She knew how to have protected sex. They'd been doing it for most of the nine years they'd been divorced.

"You had unprotected sex with Martin." Setting

a cup of decaffeinated tea in front of Olivia, Christine sat down beside her, her short brown hair and dark brown eyes a sisterly contrast to Olivia's own dark eyes and waist-length hair.

"Yes."

"And you think you're ovulating."

Hands to her mouth, she nodded. And then, lowering them, she said, "My cycle runs like clockwork."

She had to get in front of this. Not hide behind a wall of fear or acts of mental self-flagellation.

"I need levonorgestrel and I'd very much rather not approach any of my colleagues. I was hoping you could quietly hook me up with someone here…"

"You could have stopped at a clinic in LA."

Stunned, Olivia stared at her friend. She hadn't even had the thought.

Why hadn't she thought of that?

"I—" couldn't fathom the idea of walking into a clinic and seeing a doctor whose reputation she didn't know "—have to be at the women's center right after breakfast," she reminded her friend. Both of them volunteered at the local facility designed to help women suffering from domestic violence regain a sense of independence. From teaching life skills and art classes to offering counseling and financial aid, the center also offered some safe housing and took in homeless women.

Christine and Olivia did anything from teaching crafts to cooking meals. The center was where they'd met. It was where two successful, single women had found family.

"You have seventy-two hours to take the pill." Christine's soft voice filtered through the noise in Olivia's head—the cotton-like white noise that she was attempting to escape into. And fight her way out of.

"If the egg is in the fallopian tube, it could be fertilizing already and seventy-two hours from now would be in the morula stage heading toward the blastocyst stage if it wasn't already there," Olivia said. "I want it done before that happens."

It might be fertilized. But chances of that being the outcome would be less the sooner she took the pill. Not that she'd know, one way or another, so why couldn't she get the thought of ridding her body of a fertilized egg out of her head?

"Diana Louer is due in at eight. She can see you and give you the pill," Christine said. "But I'm wondering if maybe the reason you didn't go to a clinic in LA—some of which have emergency services open twenty-four hours—and maybe the reason you called me, is because a part of you is hoping that if you did make a baby last night, I might have access to some miracle that could help you bring it to life."

Olivia should never have told Christine the truth about her past—about Lily. She'd kept her secret for so long because it was the only way she could move on. And because thinking about the little girl she'd lost at just four months old hurt far too much.

"I can't gestate a healthy child," she said, hearing the way her voice hardened. Christine was just wrong on that score. Olivia was not looking for a miracle. She had no hope. None. "And I won't even take the chance," she continued. Watching the agony her tiny daughter had to endure every second of her time on earth—the permanent tubes, the tests and procedures...

Birth defects happened. She spent her days doing everything she could to ease the results of them for her own little patients. And medical results had also, in Lily's case, shown Olivia's body to be the likely cause. She had a unicornuate uterus, an abnormality meaning only half her uterus was fully formed. It hadn't allowed Lily to grow properly. She hadn't known until she was already pregnant. At only twenty years old, she'd had no cause for any kind of sonogram. And while some women with the condition delivered healthy babies, there was no guarantee birth defects wouldn't occur. To the contrary, they were at least four times more likely.

"But you want to hear about any alternatives," Christine continued, seemingly undeterred by Olivia's tone as she steadily held her gaze.

Glancing at Christine's own distended belly, Olivia said nothing. She swallowed. Started to tear up. Clasped her hands between her knees as though her legs could hold her steady.

The child Christine was carrying was biologically hers. But William wasn't. He'd been conceived in a test tube, with the egg and sperm of a married couple who'd planned to have it implanted in the woman's womb. Tragically the wife had died in an accident before that could happen. Two years later, the husband, Jamison Howe, hired Christine as a surrogate to have his baby. And they fell in love.

It was all so…romantic movie-ish.

Olivia, however, had to stay firmly grounded in real life. Was about to tell Christine so, when her friend started to speak again.

"Have you studied uterine lavage?" Christine asked the question.

"For treatment in uterine infections," Olivia said. Her specialty was neonatal pediatrics, but she was familiar with the special, catheter-type procedure.

"It's rarely done in humans anymore, but has been successfully used to remove a fertilized embryo from one woman and implant it in another. The timing is critical. Five or six days at the most and we'd have to find a surrogate for you immediately, which means we'd have to reach out to clinics who specialize in surrogacy in order to find a ready-to-go prescreened surrogate who'd be willing to take this on, and then get attorneys for both sides together immediately. But…there's a chance this could happen." When

Olivia met Christine's gaze her friend said, "If you want it to."

No.

It was too…everything. Too rushed. Too unplanned. Too out there. Too not at all what she saw for herself. Or her life. She didn't even know if she was pregnant.

She was not going to be a mother to a biological child. She'd accepted the diagnosis the day she'd buried her daughter.

"Your insurance might not cover the process, so you'd want to consider cost."

Cost wasn't an issue. Never had been. But the thought distracted her long enough to draw a full breath.

"You came here for a reason." Christine's calm tone settled around her. Not holding her, but hanging out, almost within her reach.

"You're talking about the early days of in vitro fertilization." Olivia was calm now. Fully in brain mode. "Before Louise Brown was born. She was the first official test tube baby…"

Christine was nodding. Of course, being the founder of what was becoming one of the nation's premier fertility clinics, she'd know the history of that particular medical science.

"Before they fertilized eggs in petri dishes, they were fertilized inside a woman and then transferred from that woman to a surrogate…"

"Or even to her own uterus if her fertility issues had to do with the fallopian tubes." Olivia started to shake again as two parts of herself caught up with each other.

Christine's gaze was calm. Focused. "You want to try."

"It's impossible." There was no way.

"I'd like to tell you that you've got time to think about it, but, unfortunately in your case, there is no time. If the embryo isn't transferred before it implants in your uterus, you know what you're facing."

A very difficult choice. Either terminate the pregnancy, or risk birthing another child who suffered as Lily had.

With a chest so tight she could hardly draw air, Olivia quivered from the inside out. "There might not even *be* a baby."

"You aren't willing to take that risk." Christine didn't ask. She knew.

"I don't even know of a doctor who'd be able or willing to do the procedure," she said. "With modern technology and laboratory capabilities producing such improved results, no one fertilizes in the living organism anymore."

"I know of someone who used to work with my mom," Christine said. "She lives in Europe, but is in the States on a teaching tour, so I know her license to practice here is up to date. The timing of that might not be a mistake."

Olivia's heart leaped. And left a shard of anxiety shooting through her.

Even if they could get someone to perform the procedure, the chances of extracting a healthy embryo and getting it successfully implanted in another woman were nil.

If she was even pregnant.

Christine hadn't asked her why she'd had unprotected sex in the first place, let alone when she knew she was ovulating. She had no answer to that even if her friend posed the question. Thinking back to the night before…the last thing on her mind had been her menstrual cycle. She'd been hell-bent on escaping the responsibility and caution that guided every breath she took.

Just for one night.

Not a lifetime.

"I have to talk to Martin."

Technically, she didn't. If the baby was inside her, she could make the choice. But ethically?

"Did you two ever talk about surrogacy in the past?"

She shook her head. "Ten years ago success rates weren't as good and it wasn't even legal in some places. And… I was such a mess after Lily, I couldn't imagine opening my heart to another baby, to the fact that I could lose another child. Even the idea of a surrogate miscarrying sent me into panic mode. Martin was just the opposite. He wanted to adopt right away.

He was in his thirties and the only real goal he hadn't met was having a family. He was so desperate to do that that he just wasn't thinking straight. And certainly wasn't able to understand where I was emotionally.

"And then he and I started having problems that had nothing to do with having a family. Our age difference kept popping up—I was so young, just twenty-one, idealistic, starting a career. He'd made his money and wanted to scale mountains while he was still young enough to do so. I needed to make a difference in the world, to feel like I had worth, most particularly since it seemed I'd failed at motherhood. He'd already made his difference."

"How do you think he'd react to the idea of you having his baby with the help of a surrogate?"

Shaking her head, she knew she couldn't possibly be seriously considering the idea. She was teasing herself. Playing what-ifs as though she was still a kid. "I honestly don't know," she said, because Christine was waiting for an answer to her question.

And then, thinking of Martin, she shook her head. He had his own millions but thrived on raising money for Fishnet, the licensed nonprofit he'd founded to provide supervised housing and incentives for underprivileged youth.

With another shake of her head, she said, "I can't imagine him staying in one place long enough to be part of a family."

That was partially why their odd association postdivorce had worked as long as it had. Not only were there no expectations, there wasn't even opportunity for expectations to develop. They lived in two vastly different worlds.

Marie Cove was her home.

The world was his.

Chapter Two

Martin saw the text message come in from Olivia as soon as he'd come off the golf course. He read it again in the back seat of the limo taking him to the spa where he was about to try to relax enough to enjoy a massage, and then, joined by one or two others, time in a steam room followed by cucumber cocktails in an exclusive private bar on the premises.

Call me, please?

The fact that he wanted to do so immediately, at the risk of being late for his next engagement, had him putting his phone back in his pocket.

It had taken him years to learn how to counteract Olivia's inadvertent power over him. If there were an emergency, she'd call. It's how they rolled.

The massage was a bust. Instead of relaxing into the darkened space, he spent the entire hour conjuring up various scenarios to serve as the basis for Olivia's text. She'd left something at his place and needed it before he left town was the one that won out.

She had a key. She'd never used it. Said she never would. He'd given it to her in the event that anything happened to him. There were things he wanted her to have right away, before his lawyer executed his will. Pictures of Lily, for one. He'd told her where she'd find the sealed envelope that contained the complete list of the personal items and where to find everything.

He'd give her the skin off his body if she could find happiness or comfort with it. Even before death. Anything he had, anytime…

To make up for the happiness that he hadn't been able to provide.

He hadn't been able to transform himself into a man young enough to have been able to be patient and wait out her grief before asking about adoption possibilities, or one who'd even still want children by the time she got around to being able to consider adoption.

Hell, even if he'd been able to understand the maelstrom of emotion that had emanated from her after Lily's birth. He knew grief, had experienced it firsthand and deeply even before he lost Lily—and had been suffocated by it when Lily had left them. But the only way he knew to survive the strangulating emotions, to breathe again, was to move forward.

To make a new plan.

To find another way.

Olivia hadn't been open to a new way. Nor, for

that matter, had she seemed to have all that much room for him in her grieving process, either.

The two congressmen who'd invited him to the spa joined Martin before he reconnected with his phone, and he went on to the steam room, to a private shower, a shave he didn't need performed by a lovely lady he barely noticed—a fully clothed lovely lady—and was rejoined just as he was getting his personal belongings out of the locked closet in the dressing room he'd been allotted for the afternoon. After that, socializing took precedence over the text he needed to send Olivia.

Olivia was in her office at the hospital on Saturday afternoon, halfway through her tuna sandwich from the cafeteria, when her cell rang.

Martin! The leap in her chest had to be contained. She couldn't keep overreacting to every little thing.

Slowly reaching for the phone, she saw the caller and her heart leaped again, though differently.

Christine.

She was at work to forget about her early-morning visit with her friend. She had her pill. All she had to do was swallow it. Which she was going to do just as soon as she spoke with Martin.

If she were the guy…and there was a chance a baby had been made…she'd at least want to know about the choices. To be consulted.

And maybe she was making way too big a deal

out of the whole thing. Glancing at the chart she'd just been through in preparation for stopping in to see one of her newest patients, she put her mind on the things she wanted—helping young babies in the fights for their lives—and off the things she didn't want. Make-believe internal conflicts. Drama.

She didn't want to hold on to the pain.

The fifth ring sounded. Voice mail would answer on six.

Olivia picked up the chart and, though she wasn't on duty that weekend, headed up to the unit, and her real life.

Baby V, Olivia's own moniker for the three-pound infant who'd been born the previous Thursday, was doing better than expected. Better than Olivia had even hoped. While she wasn't out of the woods, by any means, she was a strong little thing. Very little thing. She'd pretty much fit in the palm of Olivia's hand.

Back in her office, with the cell phone that had been blowing up her pocket the entire time she'd been on the unit back in hand, she was disappointed, though not surprised, to see that Martin hadn't yet answered her text. He was a busy guy. Living life to the fullest.

Doing good things.

If she called him, he'd think it was an emergency and pick up. Or excuse himself from whatever, wherever, and call her right back.

She didn't have an emergency. She had a panic attack with a slow demise.

And a friend who wasn't going to give up.

"Olivia?" Christine picked up on the first ring.

"Yeah. Sorry, I—"

"Where are you?"

"In my office, why?"

"You're at the hospital?"

Heart in her throat, Olivia sat forward in her chair, in ready mode. "Yes, why? What's wrong?"

"That's what I wanted to know! You always pick up or call me back. Always. I mean, we aren't hoverers by any means, but we pick up the phone..."

She was right.

"You weren't yourself this morning, at all. You've got a second or two to make a decision that might shape your whole life. Your mom isn't back from her cruise until tomorrow and I know she's the only other person you'd turn to. You left the center early and haven't been at your place."

Christine didn't get into flaps on a normal basis. Never, was more like it. Pregnancy hormones probably had something to do with her current, somewhat frantic state, but Olivia knew that she was partially responsible, too.

"I'm sorry," she said, settling back in her chair. "I just—"

"I know." Her friend's voice calmed immediately. They really were a lot alike, the two of them. Nur-

turers of others. Always. Truly called by their work,
naturals at what they did. Believing in what they did
as a purpose in life, not just a way to make a living.
"I was on my way to see if you were at the hospital,
since you still weren't picking up. I'm here now. I'll
be up in a few."

Pulling her thigh-length white coat more securely
around her, Olivia mostly hid the slim-fitting knee-
length beige-and-black dress she'd put on with her
favorite flat shoes after her shower that morning,
wrapping herself in what she was. A doctor.

Christine entered her office after a brief knock,
bringing the freshness of spring into that October fall
Saturday with her bright flowery dress and red shoes.

Christine always looked like she was going out to
lunch with friends. Olivia felt reserved in compari-
son. Less full of life. Though she couldn't remember
ever having felt that way around her friend, or anyone, before. It wasn't the clothes. Or the expression
on Christine's face. It was the baby bump.

Christine could birth healthy children herself.
Olivia couldn't.

Dropping her bag on one of the chairs in front of
Olivia's desk, Christine sat in the other. "How are
you?" she asked, her gaze piercing.

Olivia shrugged, pushed Baby V's folder a bit forward on the desk in front of her. Wished it was back
where it had been. Closer to her.

Baby V. A fighter. A three-pound, intensively ill, premature fighter.

Just as Lily had been.

Except that it looked like Baby V was going to make it.

There was something in that for her. A reason to cling to hope.

"Did you take it?" Christine's next question came almost right after the first. To the point.

The pill.

"Not yet." Still in the cellophane wrapper, it was in the pocket of her lab coat. Testimony to her lack of control. Her harried state.

Nodding, Christine didn't seem to pass judgment. Or take hope. The only thing emanating from her friend at the moment seemed to be concern.

Not something Olivia welcomed coming in her direction. Made her feel weak. Incapable.

Made her into the crumbling woman she'd been as she'd watched her baby girl struggle. Because her body hadn't been able to nourish her baby properly, Lily's body couldn't form normally.

"Have you talked to Martin?"

Hearing her ex's name on Christine's lips was still so odd to her. She spoke as if she knew him and she'd never met the guy. Had only known of him for such a short time.

That seemed like forever now.

Sometimes it was as though she and Christine had

somehow been connected from birth. Olivia had a lot of friends—people she associated with on a social level—but Christine was different. She'd always respected the invisible barriers Olivia had been putting up since Lily's death, and yet, somehow, seemed to see beyond them, to see what was hidden behind them. To tend to what was hidden behind them.

"I texted him. Haven't heard back yet."

Again, no judgment. Just a nod. And then, "I thought you weren't on call this weekend."

"I'm not. Just wanted to check on a new patient..." She couldn't say much. Laws prevented her from talking about her patients. Which made it easier to keep herself locked inside.

Martin used to say it was an easy way for her to keep him locked out.

Hindsight had shown her that he'd probably been right. And still, she knew she'd done what she had to do. Martin had never understood why she blamed herself for Lily's anguish. "Your body's inability to foster a fetus wasn't your fault," he'd screamed at her that last day.

Right before he'd walked out of their shared bedroom for the last time.

Christine cleared her throat and said, "I made the calls I told you I'd make."

Another pang shot through Olivia. She couldn't go back there. Had spent all day getting beyond those few moments in Christine's office that morning.

She listened, though, as Christine started to speak.

"Dr. Morrisette is willing to meet with you and, if all checks out, do the procedure. Tomorrow would work best for her."

Funny that Olivia was off the next day, as well. But there was too much to be done. A surrogate to find. Lawyers. No way this was happening that soon.

Organs were transplanted within hours of the need becoming apparent, in emergency situations, when all of the details fell into place and a life could actually be saved. But she didn't even know if there was a life to *be* saved...

"And I have a surrogate lined up to meet with you if you decide to give this a try. Beth and her husband, an EMT, have two children. The aunt who raised her and her sister is in need of a liver transplant and her sister has been cleared as the donor, but the aunt has an incredibly high deductible on her insurance and Beth can earn the money quickly enough through surrogacy. She has the family's complete support. She was due to be implanted on Monday, is midcycle and has had hormone supplements, but the couple who'd chosen her broke up a couple of days ago and have decided against having a child together. Beth would love the opportunity to meet you and is fully ready to go."

Yes, but, even assuming they found that there was an embryo forming in her one fallopian tube, they'd still need compatibility testing. Or, at the very least, to check blood types.

She knew hers and Martin's. Had records still from their attempts to help Lily… A simple check would—

"If Beth doesn't find another couple soon, her aunt's surgery will have to be canceled."

Olivia could loan her the money. Or give it to her. She didn't generally use the account Martin had set up for her during their divorce. Not anymore. Not on herself. "What does she do for a living?"

"Teaches kindergarten."

"Does the family have any pets?" She was just curious. Living alone, working long hours and being gone so much, Olivia didn't allow herself to have a fur friend, but growing up with her grandmother, who'd raised her, she'd had a houseful. Two dogs. A cat. A bird. There'd even been bunnies for a while.

"I have no idea," Christine said, her face so expressionless she gave herself away.

So this was the professional Christine her clients saw. Olivia wasn't usually so slow on the uptake.

"Tell me what you really think." The words came out as a full-out plea.

"I really don't know if she has pets."

"I mean, about *this*. What I'm doing here. What we're talking about. It's like I'm having this out-of-control moment and you're treating it all like a legitimate situation."

"This is definitely an unusual moment in time." Christine's tone didn't change, though her gaze softened, making her feel like more of the friend Olivia knew. "But sometimes that's how opportunities present themselves," she said. "You know, like winning the lottery. If you play, you could do so every week for your whole life and never hit it big. Chances are, that's what would happen. But one day, one person who's done that looks at their card, or their numbers, and they see a win. It's life changing in a second..."

Okay, the lottery. Olivia could easily focus on that.

"Today is kind of like the lottery in that your life could change for the good with one decision. The decision to buy the ticket. You might not win anything. Life might not change at all, other than you're out the money you spent trying. But you could win."

She could have a baby that was biologically hers and Martin's. A baby conceived inside of her and out of the love she held for the man she'd once married.

Having another baby wasn't a choice they'd made. Or that she'd thought to make. For nine years she'd refused to even open the door to the possibility.

For sound, valid reasons.

"You sound like you think I should take this chance."

The expression emanating from the eyes in front of her changed in the blink of Christine's eye. Professional fertility clinic owner was back. "I'm not saying that," she said, shaking her head. "This is not a decision I can make. Or even want to make."

"I see babies die on a too regular basis."

"I know you do, sweetie. And frankly, I don't know how you do what you do."

"Lily's love is how I do it," she said. "Every day I'm here, every baby I help, I'm doing what was done for Lily. And we save more than we lose. Even if we only saved one, how could I not do that?"

Christine nodded, but didn't speak up. Like she knew there was more.

Because somehow she saw what was hidden.

"I can't save them all."

"Nope."

"I don't know that I could handle having another child. I'd worry constantly. I just don't know if I'm strong enough…"

"You think all of the parents you see think they're strong enough?"

"No."

"You think that I think I'm strong enough?"

Christine had been adamant about not having another child. And then Jamie, her husband, had done some research and had introduced her to the son she'd given away during high school. The boy was happy and healthy with adoptive parents and didn't know Christine had given birth to him. But seeing that boy had changed her, helped her open her heart…

"I know you are."

"You think you're weaker than I am?"

She wasn't weak. Unless you counted weak with fear. She was *afraid*.

"Tell me something," Christine said, her hand on her enlarged belly, rubbing, and then pushing a particular spot, as though the baby was pushing against her. Olivia let the movement distract her. "You've been with me every step of the way here," Christine continued. "If not for you, I might not even have taken the chance to have William. And now look at me. I have an infant son who owns me, I'm married to a man I adore and pregnant with the child we created together. So through all of this, have you ever, even for a second, thought about having one of your eggs fertilized and using a surrogate to start a family of your own?"

Of course she had. Her own mother had thought about it and she didn't even have viable eggs to use. They'd talked about what it would be like to be in Christine's situation when she'd been pregnant with William. As a lot of women would do. Talk about it, that was.

She didn't really nod. Just a quick lowering of her chin and back up.

"And let's go at this from another angle. Do you regret having Lily?"

"Every single day. The suffering that precious little girl endured was…"

Through her tears Olivia noticed Christine shaking her head. "No decent person in this world would choose that for a baby," she said adamantly. "What I'm asking is completely different. If you had to choose between having known Lily, and having her not exist, having never had a baby, held her in your arms, known she was yours, having never known that intense motherly bond…which would you choose?"

She'd choose Lily. The answer came in a heartbeat. If she'd known how her baby was going to suffer, she wouldn't have made that choice for any reason. Period. Not for her own selfish needs or for anyone else, either. But having known that sweet soul—being a mother—seeing Lily smile when she walked in the room, knowing she was recognized and that her being there brought comfort…

"You're asking me if I'd choose to know that kind of love or not, even knowing how much it hurt to lose it."

Christine nodded. Olivia held her own counsel on that one.

"You might not be fertilizing an egg right now," Christine said. "And even if you are, the embryo might not make it through the procedure, or adhere to the uterus of a surrogate. It could get through all of that and then not thrive, resulting in a miscarriage three months from now. You know all of this. And you know I do, too. I'm not blowing sunshine here, Liv. I'm just here to help if you feel compelled to try."

Did she feel compelled to try? Seriously, what did she have to lose other than the money she'd pay Beth, which she was willing to give to this unknown angel, anyway. More, she'd always wonder if she'd killed an embryo she and Martin had conceived.

If she tried to save it, it might never flourish.

But if it was there, and she didn't try...

Suddenly, looking at the situation through Christine's eyes, things didn't seem so out of control. They seemed almost...

"Answer me this." Christine leaned forward, reaching across the desk for Olivia's hand. "If everything worked out, if the fates really are plotting here with the stars seemingly to be aligning, if Beth managed to birth a baby from an embryo inside you..." Olivia's heart leaped again. With such incredible joy, she almost didn't hear Christine's next words. "Would you want the baby?"

"More than anything in this world." There was no doubting the wealth of truth in those six words.

Chapter Three

The woman who'd been assigned the seat next to his at the formal dinner portion of Saturday night's party had long dark hair, dark eyes, tanned skin, informed conversation and a sneaky sense of humor. Victoria was single, confident…but she wasn't Olivia.

She was familiar with Fishnet, which provided boarding to young people sixteen and older who'd been drug free, held a job and attended school for at least a year straight, and then provided the financial assistance a parent might provide as long as they stayed in school—through college—and continued to meet the other criteria. The youngers had separate sleeping areas from the eighteen and olders, and had licensed caregivers—but he aimed to give the kids the same economic privileges they'd get at home if they'd had parents able to provide for them. They didn't pay rent, not as long as they were in school. And even if they went away to college, boarded there, they kept their room at Fishnet, too, so it would be waiting for them to come home to on break.

His hosts, or the party planners they'd hired, had

done their homework on him. And sat him next to exactly the type of woman who'd not only snag his interest, but intrigue him enough to make the evening memorable.

He enjoyed dinner. And the hours he spent drinking and dancing with Victoria afterward. She'd jumped right in with Fishnet statistics when he'd been procuring the promises of support for which he'd come.

Even so, he didn't invite her home with him. And declined her invitation to have a nightcap at her place. Nightcap. A nice word for sex.

As attractive as Victoria was, as close to his type as she could get, she wasn't Olivia.

And the sex he'd had with his ex-wife Friday night had been unbelievably satisfying. It was like the past ten years had been swept away and he and Olivia had been transported back to the first six months of their relationship. The first year, even. She'd been so open and giving. Fun and free and adventurous.

She hadn't even waited for him to put on a condom before she'd slid down on top of him, surprising him with her need.

For the first time in forever, her hunger had matched his.

And that was why she'd texted, asking him to call. Her version of "we need to talk." She'd had a lot to drink. Reverted back to the person she'd been before Lily.

And he realized she'd woken with regrets. He'd known it the second she'd refused coffee before dawn Saturday morning. The way she'd thrown on her clothes from the night before and hightailed it out of LA.

Back to the work that meant far more to her than his sorry old self ever had. The work behind which she hid.

He wasn't the least bit worried about repercussions from unprotected sex. In another woman, that might have been a consideration, but not with Olivia. From the moment the doctor had told them that Lily's birth defects were a result of Olivia's uterus's failure to provide proper space, his wife had changed. Blaming herself, as though she'd chosen to have a defective uterus.

Or could somehow have known that she had. She'd become obsessed with her monthly cycle. Keeping a calendar in her nightstand and on the refrigerator, too, as though to make certain that he was as aware as she was of when it was safe to have sex and when she would refuse his advances. From that point on she'd never have sex while she was ovulating...not even with a condom.

She'd apologized to him again and again for what she'd "done" to their daughter. And when he'd try to tell her it wasn't her fault, she'd shut down on him. Just as she'd done for the four months she'd spent nurturing their little girl at the hospital. Some nights she'd come home, some she wouldn't. Some she wouldn't even remember to call him and tell him she wasn't coming home.

And the nights he went up to Lily's room to be with them, she'd barely talk to him. As though she wanted him to be angry with her. To blame her. It got so bad he stopped going when she was there. Instead, he'd spend early mornings with Lily. Just talking to her. Touching her when he could.

Feeling helpless and worthless, him with all his age and experience and money and know-how, and able to do absolutely nothing to ease the suffering of one tiny, little body.

And still, she'd smiled at him. Grabbed at his finger once, even...

Olivia would be kind to him when she'd arrive before he left. His ex-wife was pretty much always kind. Just distant. And with each month that passed, the distance between them became greater.

Her walls were her protection against the pain. He understood. Just as he knew that after her loss of control Friday night, she'd need to get those walls repaired as quickly as possible.

He wasn't eager to participate in the process.

So while he didn't sleep with Victoria Saturday night, he also didn't call Olivia.

Instead, he took a shower and went to bed naked. Lying in the dark, surrounded by his ex-wife's scent, he seriously considered that it was time for him to move on. Move away.

At forty-one, he wasn't getting any younger. He needed to be with a woman who wanted to share the life he'd built. Who'd attend dinner parties so his hosts didn't feel compelled to play matchmaker, who'd enjoy traveling the world to raise money for a good cause, and meeting dignitaries in the process.

It was time to let Olivia go.

Permanently.

Olivia didn't sleep much Saturday night. Nor did she take the pill.

The longer she waited, the more chance an embryo would form, which meant more likelihood she'd be killing a living start to a baby. Her baby.

Phone in hand, she lay in bed, waiting for Martin to call. He'd have some function or other, possibly multiple functions, and then he'd call. He always did.

Martin was forty-one. His sperm might be slowing down. Could be low motility would prevent natural fertilization between them.

There was, technically, nothing stopping them from going through a normal process of fertilization—her egg, his sperm, brought together in a petri dish in a lab and implanted in a surrogate. She'd never even considered the option. Had no idea whether or not he had, either. When they'd split, she'd been unopen to any discussion about the possibility of future children.

She'd been just shy of twenty-two when Lily had died, had just completed her first year of medical school, the youngest in her class, when her daughter was born. In love, newly married and still in the process of accepting the mother she'd barely known, she'd had no realization at all that something could go so drastically wrong. No concept of how the entire course of her life could change so abruptly.

And after months of seeing her baby suffer, she'd been absolutely certain she was never going to open herself up to the possibility of that happening again. Even if she wasn't the one carrying the child.

Already a self-made millionaire, Martin had had one life goal at that point: to have a family. And she'd been adamant in her refusal to ever try again. In any fashion.

While intellectually she'd been a couple of years ahead of her age, she'd been little more than a kid— emotionally.

At thirty-two Martin had had a head start of maturity on her.

She didn't, however, think it really mature of him to not at least text her back and let her know that he was otherwise occupied and couldn't call.

Because he was with another woman? One who didn't just flit in and out of his life when one or the other of them got weak and reached out?

Part of her hoped that was the case. It would ease

the guilt she still carried where he was concerned. Martin wasn't meant to live alone.

Because of the possibility of him spending Saturday night with another woman, Olivia didn't text again. Or call him.

Instead, on Sunday morning, she dragged her thick-headed self out of bed and into the shower, and dressed in close-fitting stretch jeans, a thigh-length beige long-sleeved, fitted button-up shirt and beige knee-length boots, and was waiting on the dock in Long Beach, watching for Sylvia Miller to disembark. The cruise had been a forty-seventh birthday present from Sylvia's close friends, women who'd been her tribe since she'd left home at sixteen to go live with one of them while her mother raised the baby Sylvia had just birthed.

All of them had celebrated when she had finally been able to be a part of Olivia's life. The first couple of visits, facilitated by Olivia's grandmother when Olivia was eighteen and already in college, hadn't gone so well. Olivia hadn't been particularly open to them. But then her grandmother had died and her mother had continued to reach out. Grieving, Olivia had allowed the reconnect. She'd already been dating Martin then.

And still hadn't been all that open to the woman who'd done her own mother's bidding and stayed out of Olivia's life all the years of her growing up. Olivia's grandmother had meant well, had raised Olivia with

an abundance of love. She'd just misjudged the benefit of having one mother with one set of rules, against
the challenge of growing up with the confusion of a
grandmother and guardian with whom she lived and
a mother who was off at college and starting a life.
Mom and Grandma had made a deal. Sylvia, who had
no means to care for a child, and whose boyfriend
had relinquished all rights to the baby, would make a
life for herself with her mother's financial help, and
Grandma would raise the girl. But only if Sylvia stayed
out of the picture.

Grandma and Sylvia had failed to factor into the
equation how a little girl would feel, to know that
her own mother had abandoned her.

Standing on the dock, Olivia saw Sylvia before
her mother saw her. Noticed, immediately, the smile
on her mother's face as she spoke to the tall, gray-
haired man standing beside her. The way she looked
up to him.

Noticed, too, that not one friend was with her.

The glimpse only lasted a second. Before she'd
even started down the plank, Sylvia had stepped in
front of the man, and sped up, putting distance between them. She never glanced back. Never saw the
way the man watched her all the way down the ramp.

Could have been someone who'd merely held the
door open for her and had noticed how stunning
Sylvia still looked. Kind of odd, having a mother
who was just a few years older than her own ex-

husband. Olivia was twice the age Sylvia had been when she'd had her.

Sylvia saw her. Waved. Olivia waved back, nervous as she thought about the conversation ahead.

"You look great! Did you have a good time?" Olivia asked as her mother, letting go of the handle of the bag she'd rolled beside her, hugged her tight for a moment and then stepped back. Olivia wasn't real big on hugs. Quick and done was her modus operandi. Sylvia always respected that.

"I had a great time," her mother said, looking at Olivia with a big smile. "I missed you, though. Two weeks is too long."

"I missed you, too." She had. A lot. More than she'd ever have thought possible a decade before. "Where are the others?" she asked then, still not seeing even a single one of her mother's friends.

As she glanced toward the ship she did see the man who'd followed her mother down the plank. Alone, he was looking around, as though waiting for someone, but his gaze landed on her and Sylvia a number of times.

"We got a photo package, you know where the photographer on board takes photos of you and you can either purchase them or not at the end of the trip, and there was a mix-up. They knew you were waiting on me so told me to go ahead," Sylvia was saying, seemingly unaware that she'd caught the attention of the distinguished-looking man.

Uncomfortable, Olivia guided her mother quickly toward her white BMW and out of the guy's sight.

The last thing either one of them needed at the moment was more man trouble.

"What's wrong?" Sylvia's question had a parental note to it.

Glancing from the view, Olivia turned her attention back to her mother on the other side of the balcony table they were sharing at one of their favorite breakfast spots. They'd determined before Sylvia had left on her trip that they'd breakfast there when Olivia picked her up.

"Nothing's wrong." She looked the older woman in the eye, holding her own, and then glanced back out toward the ocean. She needed Sylvia. Loved her.

And they were still more like sisters than mother and daughter.

"A mother knows these things," Sylvia said, sipping from the tea she'd ordered. And waiting. How this woman could read Olivia so well, know her so well, when for the first eighteen years of her life they'd spent a total of three hours together, Olivia didn't know.

But she couldn't argue.

"I had unprotected sex with Martin the other night."

"And?"

"What do you mean, *and*? That's it. That's what's wrong."

"Why?"

The ocean no longer held her in its thrall. Sylvia's concerned brown gaze did that. And it all spilled out. The sadness over Christine's joy. The jealousy. Her shame for having the feelings. Drinking too much. Having sex when she was ovulating.

And Christine's offer. A solution that she wasn't going to take, but couldn't bring herself to turn down yet, either. "I'm going to give this Beth woman the money she needs for her mother's surgery." She ended with the one thing she did know for sure. "She's on hold until I give a definitive no, meaning she won't be considered by any other couples, and… I can afford to help. I *want* to help."

She'd make something good come out of her stupidity. Turn her selfish recklessness into an act of selfless giving.

"Why did you go to Christine?"

"I told you why." The pill. Why she wanted no one in her circle knowing.

Shaking her head, Sylvia watched as the table down one from them was served. Dipped her tea bag a time or two. Moved her as-yet-unused silverware a little farther out, as though making room for the plates yet to be brought to their table. They'd opted for blueberry crepes. Olivia wasn't sure she was going to be able to eat much of hers.

"You told me the reason you gave yourself." Sylvia's words came softly. "And it's valid. As it would be coming from you. But I'm just wondering if, maybe, a part of you needed to know if you had any other options. If anyone would know, it would be Christine. And if anyone could help you see that it was okay to consider those options, it would be her. After all, look at her, she brought a deceased woman's baby to life."

"Of course I wasn't looking for options…"

"Weren't you?"

What the hell? She'd needed Sylvia to tell her to grow up. To do what needed to be done. Not to analyze her. It wasn't like her mother was an expert on parenting.

"I'm not one of your clients," she said, embarrassed by the sulky tone in her voice. With a degree in counseling, Sylvia made a better than decent living working with people suffering from post-traumatic stress disorder.

"No." Sylvia nodded, her expression as serious as Olivia had ever seen it. "You're my daughter, and we're in the middle of a critical life moment here. So let me ask you this. Don't you find it a bit odd that after nine years of abstaining from unprotected sex and sex period during ovulation, you suddenly engage in both?"

"Are you seriously accusing me of doing this on purpose?"

"Of course not." Sylvia looked shocked. "If you were consciously intending to put yourself in this position, you'd spend weeks researching, another year thinking, and you'd talk to all the key players multiple times before even making a final decision."

Yeah, that sounded like her.

"So, then…"

"There's a woman inside you who's been trapped in there for a really long time." Sylvia's tone softened. "I'm thinking she's tired of all the atrophy and is fighting her way out."

"Then perhaps she should have considered consulting me. Suggesting more appropriate alternatives. Like adoption."

"Or in vitro fertilization," Sylvia said. "Odd how you didn't mention that. Like, even now, you're trying to shut her up."

"Seriously, Sylvia, I'm not one of your clients."

"And in response to your earlier statement, I'm guessing she, you, didn't 'consult' you as you say, because you turned off her volume years ago. You took away her voice. And in so doing, lost your chance to spend a year or more making a decision that she's chosen to make."

"I still have that choice." She always had choices. She could take the pill right then if she wanted to. It was in her purse. And she could think about in vitro fertilization if she ever decided she wanted to do so.

What she didn't want to think about was what her mother had just said. Didn't want to know if there was real truth in the words, or just a guess that fell short.

"Why are we even having this discussion?" Olivia

asked, looking the other woman in the eye, one-on-one, equal to equal, not child to parent. She'd never been this woman's child. Only her baby. And then her adult offspring. "What does it matter why I did what I did Friday night or Saturday morning? What matters is feeling good about taking the pill. Knowing that it's the smart choice."

She wanted Sylvia to sit there with her while she swallowed it.

"It matters because it has bearing on what you do from here," Sylvia said softly, leaning forward. "If your inner self is crying out, Liv, you might need to give her this chance. It could be the only way you're ever going to know real joy again—if she forces you."

"You make me sound like I have multiple personalities."

"Nope, just one. But we all have different sides of ourselves. It seems like you live all on one side. And you can go on living half-alive. Nothing or no one is going to stop you if that's your choice. But I think your other half is trying hard to give you a shot at more. Even if you go ahead with this plan, and it doesn't work out, at least you've walked through the door she forced open."

And if she took the pill…was she stepping back out and closing that door forever? Because of what the choice said about her inability to open her heart to wild chances?

"You think I should do it. I should see the doctor, have the procedure and see if anything transpires from it?"

The shake of Sylvia's head was the only response she got as a young man approached their table with a tray bearing two plates. He set them down, asked if they wanted anything else and left, seemingly oblivious to the life-changing conversation taking place right in front of him.

Olivia could hardly breathe as she waited for him to leave. For her mother to explain why she'd just shaken her head. Like if Olivia called Christine and actually tried to move forward with this off-the-wall scheme, she'd be doing something wrong.

"I think you need to be honest with yourself," Sylvia said as soon as the waiter was out of earshot. "You need to admit that you really want this chance. Or you need to face the fact that you don't. This isn't about making a choice, Liv. Or listing pros and cons. It's about listening. Inside. On some level you know what you really want, and you're also fighting it. Stop fighting. Listen to your heart. Let it speak to you. And then do what you need to do, what you can do, to give it what it needs."

In that moment, with those words, Olivia felt like she and her mother had just found home.

Chapter Four

Martin spent the entire flight to Italy on the phone with lawyers and investors, doing what he could to save a deal with the city of Philadelphia for an abandoned apartment building that would allow Fishnet to open up a branch in a spot where it was so critically needed. If he didn't get things ironed out before Monday, the whole thing was going to fall apart.

He wasn't about to let that happen. And by the time he landed, he had achieved his goal. He'd saved the deal.

Before he deplaned, he did one more thing.

He texted Olivia and let her know that they could talk when he got home. Less than twenty-four hours from when her message had come in and it had sat there, feeling like a lifetime to him. Ignoring her took that much effort.

He was back in LA on Thursday. They could talk when he got back.

She'd be in his life until then.

And then he was done. Had to be. He didn't want to spend his life alone, traveling alone, returning to a home he shared with no one. He didn't want to be set up with interesting women he didn't know, or dance with beautiful strangers as partners for the rest of his life.

He knew what he wanted. What he needed. A wife. Someone who wanted to share his world. To want him to share hers. And Olivia, with her career and small-town life, just didn't fit.

Truth was, he didn't fit her, either. He really never had. He'd wanted the small-town life when he'd thought he'd be raising a family, but at forty-one, neither appealed anymore. And while she'd adored Lily, had wanted Lily, Olivia would really have been happier finishing her degree before starting a family. Maybe, if he hadn't forced things, the pregnancy would have been more successful. He'd done his own studying in the years since they'd lost Lily. Women with unicornuate uteruses could have normal pregnancies, birthing children without defects. Maybe if Olivia had been just a little bit older, if her uterus had had more time to grow into itself, to strengthen…

And those maybes…he couldn't do anything about them. But he could move on.

He'd lost more than ten years of his life loving the wrong woman. He couldn't afford to waste any more.

Sundays were supposed to be a day of rest. At least when she wasn't on call. Instead, there she sat in a room with comfortable, pale yellow couches, two windows, a coffee table, her mother, Christine and Dr. Rose Morrisette, the expert conducting the procedure. They were all looking at her.

Were all there because of her.

Hardly able to wrap her mind around everything rushing through it, Olivia recognized preliminary signs of emotional shock.

And was having some clear thoughts, too.

"So what did you think?" Christine, seated across from her with Dr. Morrisette beside her, asked the question. All three pairs of eyes, Sylvia's from right beside her, were focused on her.

Being the star of the show wasn't a place she usually occupied. Or wanted. And yet, there she was.

And a picture came to mind of the athletic-looking blonde woman who'd just left the room with her husband. Brian Applegate, an EMT, had completely supported his wife's choice to help her aunt by using her body to give someone else a chance at life.

"I liked them," Olivia said. If she'd met them in another time or place, she might not have noticed them, but had felt instantly drawn to them. To Beth.

Because she'd needed to be?

"I just feel bad, getting their hopes up, taking up all of your time when I'm still not…"

She'd heard from Martin. He was in Italy. Said they'd talk when he got back on Thursday. By then it would be too late. Too late to take the pill. Too late to get an embryo out of her body and into one where it could have a chance of survival.

If she waited until Thursday, and was pregnant, she'd have no option but termination.

The thought of that made her want to curl up and die.

"Their kids are with her sister and they're getting a minivacation," Christine said, still speaking about Beth and Brian. "They're going to the beach this afternoon. I gave them suggestions for dinner downtown."

She nodded. Got the message behind Christine's words. Everyone had choices. Everyone. Christine, her mother, even Rose, were in that room, spending Sunday afternoon with her, because they chose to do so.

And Olivia had the freedom to make whatever decision she chose, too.

"I'll pay for their room, and their meals, too," she said.

"They didn't ask for that, at this point, but if you choose to go through with the embryo transfer, it will all be covered in the legal agreement."

The room fell silent then. A silence filled with waiting.

"They were particularly moved by your story," Christine finally said softly. "Beth said that of all the profiles she's read over the past couple of months, she'd choose you to surrogate for first."

Clasping her trembling fingers together, Olivia pursed her lips. Nodded.

"Maybe you don't really want this, sweetie," Sylvia said from beside her. Still in the jeans she'd worn off the boat, her suitcase in Olivia's truck, her mother hadn't even been home yet.

And had just pissed her off, too. Sylvia was her parent. She should know what Olivia really wanted and to say that she didn't want—

Her brain put a halt on the thought right there. Just as it had been fighting the soul-searching her mother had encouraged her to do over breakfast.

She needed to think. She needed to talk to Martin. She needed time.

And didn't have it.

"The chance of success, assuming there is a blastocyst when we get there, is still not great," Rose Morrissette spoke up. While easily in her sixties, the black-haired woman was an imposing figure. She'd made studying fertility her life's work and knew its history well. Her list of percentages and possibilities would have made Olivia's head swim, if she even had room for it all.

Olivia listened. Focused somewhat. And when the other woman fell silent, said, "But there's still a chance that it would work."

"Absolutely. Though if we were to proceed I'd need you to sign a legal document stating that you're fully aware that the chances aren't in your favor. Most particularly since this type of thing isn't generally done anymore. When we, as a medical profession, moved to laboratory fertilization, the success rate rose exponentially, so we've never looked back."

And if Olivia were planning to have a child, that's the way she'd go. Laboratory. Petri dishes. Modern science. But she didn't have that plan.

She had a possibly fertilized egg inside her, traveling toward a uterus that would hurt it.

"Although I read on the way over here that it is commonly done that way in cattle and horses with good success," Sylvia piped up beside her.

Glancing at her mother, it hit Olivia that Sylvia had a real stake in this. The fact that it was only now fully occurring to her was a testament to her state of mind.

If she did this, and it worked, her mother would be a grandmother. Sylvia had never met Lily, as only parents had been allowed in to see her. Yet she'd been the one to nurse Olivia through the devastating loss.

"There's also no guarantee insurance would cover the procedure." Christine dropped the words into the room, where sun shone in through the windows and all else seemed surreal to Olivia.

"Most probably not," Dr. Morrisette said, adding, "though depending on how we charge it, it might. If you do nothing and end up pregnant, we'd need to go in, anyway."

Olivia didn't care about the insurance. The percentages. Or cows.

She cared about giving any possible baby inside her the chance to live. Period.

There.

Just like that.

The truth was set free.

Olivia tried to call Martin Sunday night. He didn't pick up. A few minutes later she had a text from him, asking if there was an emergency.

It took her another fifteen minutes to decide that there wasn't. And told him so.

She'd made up her mind. Talking to him at that point was more formality, decency, than anything else, and not something to be done over the phone across continents. Most particularly not with their history.

And when he asked if they could talk on Thursday, she demurred.

If no viable embryo was recovered, if Beth's body didn't accept it if there was, there was no reason for Martin to know she'd even tried. No reason to open the huge problematic conversation. Or awaken the hurt and frustration he'd felt when she'd refused to consider other options for having a child nine years before.

She was currently one year younger than he'd been way back then. Their perspectives would always have that distance between them.

Not that he'd given her any indication at any time in at least the past five years that he still had an interest in raising a family. His life had broadened since then. The scope of his goals had changed.

Most of that night, she didn't let herself think about her ex-husband. Or any baby they'd conceived. Past or present. She thought a lot about Baby V. About the man she'd seen looking at her mother, and Sylvia's seeming to not really remember what she was talking about when she'd questioned her mother about it.

She thought about Christine and Jamie. About the son they had, the second one on the way and how, though it was odd that William belonged to Jamie's deceased wife, they were really making it work.

Love was making it work.

And on Monday morning, as she donned a simple gray formfitting tweed skirt, matching T-shirt and flat gray shoes, she made herself go over, again and again, her schedule at the hospital later that day. Sylvia had offered to spend the night with her. To travel with her to Christine's clinic first thing that morning, where Beth and Dr. Morrisette were meeting her to perform the procedure. She'd declined. She truly had just wanted to be alone.

At home, and on her drive to the clinic. She'd found a serene safe place inside and had to stay there.

As she approached the clinic door, she thought about what was immediately ahead. There'd be some lab work done. A technician was on call for that, too. They only had a matter of hours from the time any embryo was removed from her before it would have to be implanted in Beth. There'd probably be some cramping. Because she had to be at work that afternoon she'd opted out of any kind of medication to make her more comfortable. Beth, bless her heart, would need to remain supine for a while.

Christine, in a flowing, deep purple dress, greeted her at the door of the clinic.

"You okay?" she asked.

Olivia didn't speak. But she nodded. She had her truth and had to act on it. There was nothing else.

The procedure was similar to other gynecological visits. Clinical. An internal flushing. Dr. Morrisette, other than checking in on Olivia's comfort level, spoke only to the nurse assisting her. At one point Olivia was aware of intense cramping, but didn't care. She was aware when the material was out of her body and being hurried away. Knew asking questions was pointless. The naked eye wasn't going to tell them anything.

Dr. Morrisette finished up quickly after that. And after pulling the paper sheet over Olivia and telling her she could sit up, she smiled for the first time since she'd entered the room.

"It went like clockwork, Doctor," she said, throwing her gloves in the trash. "You can get dressed, and your part is done here."

She was done.

Either way. There was no more need for her or her body to be present. Beth was the one whose journey was only starting. Possibly for nine months.

The idea was eerie. Leaving Olivia feeling... incredibly empty.

She dressed quickly as soon as she'd been left alone. Grabbed her purse, the black one, she noticed, not the gray one that went with the day's shoes, and frowned. She should have paid more attention. Now she'd have to carry around an unmatching purse for the rest of the day.

The thought brought tears to her eyes. Swiping at them didn't seem to help so she reached for a tissue, which caused her leg to bump into the hard, plastic chair close to the table, and so she fell into it. Rubbed at her leg. And cried some more.

She might have sobbed all day, or maybe for the rest of her life, if Christine hadn't come in. The second she heard the doorknob turn, she sat up. Wiped her eyes.

"Hey." Christine's tone was soft as she kneeled beside her. "It's okay," she said inanely. Followed by, "Do you need something for pain, after all?"

No pill was going to help this. The bump on her leg didn't even hurt anymore. If it ever had. She couldn't be sure and reached for another tissue.

"Talk to me, Liv. There's still time to stop this,"

Christine quickly added. "Beth's here and being prepped, but it's not too late."

They'd signed all the paperwork the evening before. With two different lawyers present. One representing her, and one representing Beth.

"What's wrong?"

Olivia met Christine's gaze, saw the concern there, and realizing she was the cause of it, said, "My purse doesn't match my shoes..." at which time the tears started again.

Sitting back on her haunches, Christine watched her.

And Olivia couldn't pretend that she was okay.

"It's gone," she whispered.

"What's gone?"

"The baby. If there is one...

"I had it inside me.

"For two whole days.

"And now I don't."

Each sentence ended with a need for air. A moment to catch her breath and hold back tears.

"I'm empty," she finished. It was stupid to feel this way. Unexpected.

And so real she wasn't sure she could get up and walk out of that room.

"It's a little like losing Lily all over again..."

Which made no sense. She'd never been a drama queen.

"Except that it's not gone," Christine told her.

"They already got a look, Liv. You were right to be concerned. Right about everything. There's a viable embryo."

A jolt passed through her. Excitement shot one way. Anxiety another. "There is?" she asked through her tears. Let everything just drip down her face as she stared at Christine.

"Dr. Morrisette was going to tell you, but I asked if I could."

Nodding, Olivia stared at Christine, trying to see the truth in her dark brown eyes. Something that would make it all real.

Trying to understand the ramifications.

"I did the right thing," she said, "being concerned. If I'd ignored myself, I'd be…"

Relief washed over her. And as it dissipated, Christine said, "So this is it, Liv. We can move forward or not. It's your call."

Looking Christine dead in the eye, she answered immediately. "There is no call to make," she said. "If there's even the remotest possibility that my baby can live, I have to give it that chance."

"You'll be a single mother, changing your entire life overnight."

She nodded. Almost dizzy with the magnitude of the spins her life had taken in the past forty-eight hours. "Yeah, I've got a lot to think about, and might soon have major plans to make, but I've got time to make them, too."

"You want this." It wasn't a question that time.

Nodding again, Olivia smiled and teared up again. "I do," she said. "I really do."

And in that moment, nothing else mattered.

Chapter Five

All day Monday Martin told himself it was good that Olivia had opted not to reply. She'd taken his hint in not immediately responding to her plea for a conversation. She knew him. Probably realized that he was done.

Hell, she'd probably set the whole thing in motion and was still dragging him along with her little finger. That scenario explained the incredible, out-of-character sex on Friday night. She'd been saying goodbye.

And he'd responded accordingly.

Giving her what she wanted. To be away from him.

Out of his life for good.

After speaking at a conference, he'd gone on to the preplanned cocktail hour with some of the nation's wealthiest people, and then to dinner. He was feeling great. On top of his game.

And avoided all conversation that could in any way turn flirty. He didn't feel flirty.

He felt like he'd been dumped by his wife.

Again.

* * *

Olivia had just finished her last rounds late Tuesday afternoon, had managed to have a few hours that felt almost normal, when her cell buzzed a text.

From Martin.

I'm in Marie Cove. Would like to speak with you. Will wait until you're available.

What if she wasn't available at all that night? She was teaching a hygiene session at the center from six to seven. Women who attended earned points that they could spend in the thrift shop for things ranging from used clothing and houseware items to canned goods and laundry detergent. If she didn't give the session, they lost an opportunity to earn their points.

She'd planned to have dinner with Christine afterward—something they used to do regularly after center sessions, and hadn't done quite as often since her friend's marriage.

But...

Why aren't you in Italy?

It was Tuesday, not Thursday.

I need to speak to you.

Her heart started to thud. At forty-one Martin

was decades away from old, but it wasn't completely unheard of for men in their forties to develop heart problems...

What's wrong?

When's a good time for you to meet?

If there's something wrong with you, you need to tell me now. Is it your heart?

Sending a quick plea to the gods that it was nothing life-threatening, she stood in her office, staring at the phone as she awaited his response. She had to finish charting. But if it was an emergency...

He wouldn't be texting her. Or be willing to wait until she was available.

So much for normalcy. Apparently bouts of idiocy were still in her system.

In spite of how empty she'd felt after her procedure the previous day.

Just had a physical last week. Everything in normal range. Doc says I'm going to live to be a hundred.

Olivia sat down, just glad to know that he was okay. He might not be the right partner for her, but she still cared about him. Always would.

She texted Christine. Asked if she could take a rain check on dinner. Explained that Martin was in town.

And then she texted Martin back again.

I'll be home by seven thirty. You're welcome to stop by.

Whatever it was he had to tell her probably wouldn't be nearly as earthshaking as her news.

With a couple of wine coolers in the refrigerator, Olivia tried to convince herself she was prepared for Martin's knock on the door of her luxury condominium overlooking the Pacific Ocean. She'd left his name with the doorman. Knew he wouldn't be late.

She had refused to change out of the black-and-white tweed short-sleeved dress and black flats she'd worn to work and on to the center that day. Her hair was down from its bun, freshly brushed and hanging down her back, but mostly because it had started to fall and she hadn't wanted to bother putting it all back together again.

At 7:25 she thought about a wine cooler. Would have preferred to open one and have it to sip on during the upcoming conversation, but considering that a drink with Martin had gone all haywire the last time she'd seen him, she knew she had to wait for that small bit of relaxation until after he'd been and gone.

Was she going to tell him about the live embryo? About Beth? The implantation?

The question had been rolling around in her mind

since she'd received his text. With varying results. If he cared, wanted the baby, they could share the tumultuous time of waiting the ten days until Beth's first pregnancy test.

What was she doing?

Creating some kind of fantasy about her and Martin finding each other again through an unplanned pregnancy was just plain stupid.

Impractical.

And dangerous.

Their problems weren't going to be solved by bringing a child into the mix. If anything, they'd only be amplified. The way he'd approach parenthood would be different at forty-one than it had been a decade earlier.

What if he insisted that she quit her job? He'd certainly done his best to talk her out of medical school. Putting family first, he'd called it.

But the man's genes were in a live embryo. He had a right to know.

What if the embryo was no longer alive? What if it didn't adhere to Beth's uterus? Then he had nothing, and therefore, no need to know about it…

It wasn't like there were any decisions that needed to be made, or even any plans that couldn't wait ten days. On the contrary—she had to wait.

His knock came at 7:28 and she was glad she wasn't holding the wine cooler. She might have dropped it.

She was a nervous wreck and needed to get over herself. Be the person she'd worked so hard to grow into over the past decade.

In black jeans and an off-white button-up shirt with the sleeves rolled up his forearms, with that tiny bit of silver starting to show in his pitch-dark hair, Martin filled her space before he'd even walked through the door. He was just one of those guys who looked like something off a movie set. His body, yes, the long legs and confidence with which he walked, but it was those vivid blue eyes and the expression on his face, too. The one that made you feel like you were the only person in the world he wanted to be with in that moment. Like you were that special.

No one was that special. Not all the time.

With hardly a smile, she led him to the balcony directly off from the dining room. They'd taken morning coffee there once when he'd come to town a couple of years before to deliver some papers and had ended up in bed together. She'd already turned on the small lamp on a side table by the wicker couch to offset the darkness.

And yet leave them surrounded by shadows, too. That seemed safer somehow.

"You want some tea? Or bottled water?" she asked.

Shaking his head, he took a seat in one of the two wrought-iron chairs set at the little table. She'd have preferred her wicker rocker next to the couch, but whatever.

"What's up?" she asked, missing that wine cooler again. For something to do with hands that couldn't sit still in her lap. And for a little assistance with relaxing the nerves that seemed to be standing up and screaming throughout her body.

He didn't answer right away. Clasped his hands, lifted them to the table, dropped them to his sides. At least they had that in common—their hands seemed to be malfunctioning.

"How would you describe our relationship?" he finally asked, throwing her completely off course. Whatever she'd been expecting, it hadn't been that.

Not sure where he was going with it, or why, she thought carefully about her answer. "We're divorced," she said, speaking slowly. "And amicable."

He watched her and she couldn't tell if she'd gotten the answer right. But had a feeling there'd been a right way to answer—something that would have given him what he was looking for.

"We care about each other," she said, continuing to talk. Not wanting to disappoint him. Searching for the truth within her.

And struggling to get beyond her immediate internal crises long enough to find peace on any other matters. But she kept trying. Because it seemed that important to him.

"We know we aren't right for each other," she said next. "We want different things and, on a daily basis, those differences build resentments that tarnish the good stuff."

Lips pursed now, he cocked his head, still watching her.

Either she'd hit the nail on the head or she'd horribly missed and hit a nerve.

"I consider you a friend," she inserted quickly, going for the positive aspects. "A *close* friend. One of those I'd call in times of need."

The secret she held made her uncomfortable as she delivered the last, but…she had texted him. Asked him to call. He'd declined.

She'd figured he was ending whatever it was they still had.

Had even considered that maybe she'd wanted him to do so…

And started to get a bit miffed. He was the one who'd said *he* needed to talk. Why was she the only one doing so?

"What about you? How do you view us?"

He seemed to give the matter real thought. Continued to study her, as she was assessing him. Eye to eye. Just as they'd always done.

"Much like you do," he finally said.

So she'd gotten the answer right?

Where did that leave them? Where was he going with it?

Should she tell him about the embryo? The procedure?

With him sitting there, meeting her gaze so openly, she wanted to. Badly.

He wasn't just a friend. In some ways he was her best friend. The one she trusted to have her back more than any other.

One whose back she'd die to protect.

She needed to tell him.

Just as soon as he got what he'd come for. Or told her what he'd come to say. She wasn't sure which it was at that point.

If he was in need of some kind of reassurance…

"What do you expect from me?" His question stunned her. She and Martin didn't ask those kinds of questions, hadn't since their divorce.

"Nothing," she said, thinking back to try to figure out what had prompted this discussion. To remember anything she'd said or done to make things go wrong between them recently.

She'd texted him and asked him to call. Hadn't thought anything of it.

But maybe…she hadn't been herself over the weekend to be sure… Should she have not texted? She'd made her choice without his input, which meant she really hadn't needed it. Maybe that was it… She'd been out of line contacting him or seeking his call back. She'd just been in such a state…thinking he had a right to know what she was contemplating.

And as it had turned out, she'd done just fine on her own.

Not really on her own. She'd had family, a best friend, others who'd been with her.

She'd done it without him.

So…had she been too needy with that text? She used to be, where he was concerned. Or felt she had been, at any rate. At twenty-one she'd felt his decade on her had made him seem so smart to her. So knowing. Like she could rely on his advice more.

Ridiculous when you considered that she was in medical school at twenty-one. But intellectual advancement didn't mean that one was emotionally more mature. She just wasn't sure what they were getting into. Where it was all going to lead.

Had no real idea where she even wanted it to lead.

Because, other than her work, she hadn't dared to want anything for a long time. The thought struck her cold. He was still watching her. Almost as though he could read the thoughts playing through her mind. She wasn't alarmed by the idea. Maybe he'd find what he was looking for.

"You really think you have no expectations," he said as more and more outside lights came on around them in the darkness. Seeming to encompass them even more closely in their little sphere.

"I expect you to treat me decently," she said. "To be honest with me. Why? Do you think I'm expecting too much of you?"

She'd been needy nine years before. Her baby had

just died. But surely he'd seen how much she'd grown
up. She wasn't that kid anymore…

The shake of his head was almost sad. Like he
was saying no to something that had mattered to
him. Which didn't make nearly enough sense to her.

"I'm not at all sure it's you," he said, confusing
her further.

"What, then?"

Martin held her gaze for another few seconds and
then looked away. Leaning his elbows on his knees,
he stared out toward the lights along the shore, or
those of boats bobbing out in the dark beyond.

"I'm too… It's too…"

"Too what?" He was scaring her.

"You have this weird pull over me," he told her,
glancing sideways at her. "It's like you've still got me
wrapped around your finger and all you have to do
is tug and there I go, off to wherever you drag me."

Wow. She hadn't expected that. Wasn't even sure
what to make of it.

Was he blaming her for his feelings?

Was she causing it?

Was he asking her to stop?

How did she stop what she didn't know she was
doing?

Or…

"Maybe it's just a product of who we are," she said
softly, finding a strange sense of calm. "We've been
through so much, Martin. Stuff that we'll never get

over. That bond will always be there, even though we aren't together…" As she talked, she felt stronger. Her words grew bolder. Her need to speak with him that weekend while she wrestled with what to do, even her heading to him in LA when the sadness and jealousy were getting to her—they were all part of it. "I feel it with you, too," she told him, wondering what it meant. That they were having this conversation. That he'd started it.

Was it unbelievable that she'd thought they'd ever find their way back to being in each other's lives?

"Take tonight, for instance. I'm sitting wondering why you called," Olivia continued. "Wondering what you need from me. Worrying whether or not I'm giving it to you…"

When he sat back, he didn't look happy.

His nod seemed…final.

"I'd already come to the conclusion that what we're doing isn't healthy," he said, his words like stakes in her heart. "After hearing what you just said, I'm even more convinced."

"What are you saying?" She didn't want to know. But her need to know was stronger than any desire to cover her ears.

"I think we need to do what we should have done nine years ago, Liv. What we said we were doing when we divorced. We need to break this invisible tie that's holding us back from getting on with our lives. We need to let each other go."

Chapter Six

It took everything Martin had to stay seated, calmly watching the stricken expression that crossed Olivia's beautiful face. For a second he started to panic. Like he was making a mistake. But only for a second. Reason returned almost instantly and he knew he had to be strong.

Not just for him, but for her, too.

"If we were meant to be together, Liv, nine years wouldn't have passed with us still here, in this same place. We'd have found our way back to each other." That fact, along with others, had occurred to him on the long flight back from Italy the night before. He'd slept some. Enough. And made calls to apologize for the emergency that had come up that required him to cancel some engagements. And left it to his administrative assistant, Barbara, a woman ten years his senior who'd been with him since his dot-com days, to handle things. Happily married and a grandmother now, she rarely traveled with him, but was the absolute best at keeping him on track.

She knew him. And better than that, she understood his goals. Shared them, even. That's what he wanted in a mate, too. Someone who shared his goals. Someone whose goals he could share.

"I've built a life, filled with important work, that really fulfills me. I never knew how much I'd thrive on traveling all over the world. Seeing life from differing perspectives. Meeting so many interesting people. Helping at-risk kids make lives for themselves. I look forward to the day when I get up in the morning. I'm excited about the future. The only thing missing is someone to share it with me."

Her gaze didn't waver. Her lips did. As though he was hurting her. He hadn't meant to. Hadn't wanted to.

"Are you happy?" he asked then as some wayward thought struck him that maybe she'd be open to filling the newly forming, or at least newly acknowledged, open position in his life. "Here in Marie Cove? Being a doctor? Working in the NICU?" Could it be that he'd missed something? That she'd served whatever penance she'd felt she owed and would be willing to move on?

"I am." There were tears in her eyes, but certainty in her voice, too. "I love what I do, Martin. And I love my life. My friends. My mother… I spent the first eighteen years of my life without her. More than that, really, since I wasn't thrilled with her when she first showed up. She moved here to be close to me. Got a job here to be close to me. Mostly, though, every single time I save a baby's life…it's like a spiritual thing… I can't not be there…"

She was sealing their fate. He knew it. And knew she did, too.

Nothing between them had changed. She put her career first, and he wouldn't come second again. She wanted to live her life in one spot, and he didn't want to travel the world alone. She was stuck in place and he was running…

"Who knows where I'll be a year from now," she continued, but he held up a hand, shaking his head. He wasn't open to the "who knows what the future will bring" speech again. He'd heard it nine years before. And since then, too. He didn't have another ten years to wait around and find out. He'd turned forty the year before. Had already let go of any desire to be a father, raise a family. Had made peace with that. Had actually seen that it was for the best. But he couldn't let his need to be with her talk him out of anything more.

"I've realized that our…various liaisons with each other…they're keeping us from finding any kind of lasting relationship anywhere else," he said, maybe a little too harshly.

"You don't want to have sex anymore." Her tone gave nothing away, and for a moment Martin longed for the young woman he'd married whose emotions dressed every word she spoke.

"Do you think we can meet for an occasional dinner, or, say, even the passing of documents that need to be signed quickly, without having sex?" His reference to the last time he'd been in her condo was finally out. He'd come to town to get her signature on an investment return document; she'd invited him to share the omelet she'd just taken out of the pan. They'd made it until a final cup of coffee on the balcony, where he'd kissed her. The sex they'd had that morning had been rushed and decadent, with both of them throwing clothes back on hastily to make it to work on time, and the memory had been sitting right there with him since she'd led him to the balcony.

He'd even gone so far as to wonder if she'd led him out there on purpose. To remind him of that morning. To further keep him around. Or remind him that they couldn't be trusted alone together.

The warring thoughts convinced him more than anything it was time to end things between them. Not because Olivia had any perverse or controlling motive, or even desire to have any hold on him, but because his caring for her made him vulnerable to her. Made him unsure of himself. Of her.

A woman who wasn't right for him. A woman he wasn't right for. He'd hurt her as badly as she'd hurt him. Maybe more. He didn't negate that.

The fact that she hadn't answered his question didn't go unnoticed. She didn't answer because she knew they couldn't keep a promise to not have sex.

They'd already tried. More than once. They'd failed. And that fact left them no other choice.

"I'm forty-one, Liv. I don't want to grow old alone. Or even live alone anymore. I want a partner, and half of my life is gone." He couldn't ask a woman to share his world and step aside occasionally when his ex-wife was around.

Which meant that if he couldn't resist the temptation to touch Olivia, and vice versa, if they couldn't resist the passion that was always present between them, then they had to stay away from each other. Period.

He promised himself the sadness that was cutting a gaping hole in his gut would pass.

"Do you have to leave? Shouldn't we talk about this?" Olivia followed Martin past the dining room, through her open-spaced living room and to the porcelain-tile entryway by her front door. She didn't want him to go, reached out a hand to touch his back, but pulled her hand in before she made contact.

Her news trembled on the tip of her tongue. And yet…what news was there? Only possibilities. It would keep him from walking out on her. She was as certain of that as she was that she'd take her next breath.

Was it fair to play with him that way?

If Beth ended up pregnant, Olivia would have to tell him. Not legally, maybe, because he wasn't on the surrogate agreement—wasn't going to be named on the birth certificate. But she'd have to tell him.

Still, she couldn't use a baby to hold him to her, even then. It wouldn't be healthy for any of them.

"What if we tried again?" The question came with hesitation. But it would be better to have the conversation before they knew whether or not they had a baby in the picture, so they'd know they didn't make choices based on the child.

Except she knew there was a possibility. So was she asking the question *because* of the baby, or because he'd just broken up with her?

Again.

Forcing her to fight... The thought came and hung suspended while another presented: fight for what? What did she want from him?

"Should we try to come up with some kind of compromise?" she asked, looking for answers that she knew weren't there. She just couldn't stop looking, and that meant something, didn't it?

Turning at the door, he stood, less than a foot away, staring straight into her eyes. Maybe if they met eye to eye, rather than him towering several inches over her, she wouldn't feel so...protected by him.

She didn't need protection. Didn't even want it.

"When I met you, I thought I'd already reached the pinnacle of my professional success," he told her. "The thrill was gone. I was thirty years old and I'd done everything I'd ever hoped of doing. I'd made my mark on the world, and I'd made all the money I'd ever need," he said, not telling her anything new, but telling it in a way that felt new.

She soaked in his words. Needing more.

"The only thing left that gave me any sense of anticipation, of looking forward to the years ahead, was having children. My parents had nothing monetarily, but what we had was more valuable than any wealth will ever be. The emotional riches they gave me... I wanted to pass those on. And to have a family life that wasn't fraught with financial distress."

Her heart thumped. She almost blurted out that he might still be able to have that...

"Then you walked into that room, and the minute I saw you, and caught you looking at me, the world was brand-new again. It's like I suddenly had everything to do. And a lifetime to look forward to."

She'd felt the same way. He'd been a guest lecturer at a professional technology seminar she'd attended, or rather, one of many she'd been encouraged to choose from, her senior year in college. Everyone had raved about the lecturer, and as little interest as she had in the underbelly of the computer world, she figured it was worth paying the extra money to attend his seminar as she'd have a better chance of staying awake.

"It's the spark," she said softly, holding his gaze. "That thing that lights you up enough to get you out of bed in the morning…to give you strength when times are hard…"

He nodded. "Everyone needs a purpose."

Such simple, overused words, and yet…they were everything.

"When you got pregnant so soon, I knew it was the seal on the choice we'd made," he continued. "Validation and promise all rolled into one." The half smile on his face as he appeared to look back took her back, too, reminding her of how great they'd been together.

How sexy he'd been since the first moment she'd seen him in that theater-style auditorium crowded with students and faculty.

The flame of desire started low in her belly once again and spread like the fire it was. She leaned in without thought, expecting a kiss, and did a mental regroup before anything happened.

Whether he'd been aware, under the spell with her, she didn't know. But thought so. And took heart.

"After Lily died…it all changed."

"Not all of it." They still wanted each other. They'd always wanted each other.

"How do you feel about traveling?" he asked, his gaze more piercing after her last comment.

She shrugged. "I'm not opposed to it. You know, in a few years, maybe. When I've got more experience under my belt I'd love to travel and teach others what I'm learning in the NICU. We're a small hospital, but being so close to the California universities, we're getting to see a lot of the newest technologies and practices. We've got a baby now who was born just over a pound and she's thriving…" She heard the rise of excitement in her voice, saw the way his eyes closed for too long to be a blink and stopped.

"I want to travel," she said. But not yet.

And it wasn't just about that.

"You don't want a wife who's an equal," she said, words she'd never said to him before. "You want a wife who wants what you want, who supports what you want, but not one who wants things for herself."

"I need a woman who wants for herself, needs for herself, the same kinds of things I need and want."

What did she say to that? As usual, he made sense. He always made so damn much sense.

"I'm a specialized pediatrician who's respected in my field and yet you make me feel almost like a kid again," she said. "And not in a good way. When do you ever see that I know as much as you do, Martin?"

"You're a doctor, Liv! You've been through medical school. You know far more than I do," he told her, frowning.

"And yet…you're the one who's ready to walk away from us. Is that healthier?"

"Do you think it's not?"

She wanted to think it. And had no valid reason for the wanting. Except that she might be having a baby, through an angel named Beth, and if she was, Martin was the father.

Which was no reason for them to continue trying to fit together when they didn't.

Martin was right. She knew he was.

And hated that she hadn't seen it first. Or at least at the same time.

It had always been a problem with them. He'd made her feel warm and loved, turned on as hell, but always like a bit of a kid, too. Her with no daddy in her life.

"My mother told me a few years ago that she thinks I feel for you as some kind of father figure... that I had, as she put it, 'daddy issues.'"

He didn't seem taken aback by the statement. Or even surprised. "Do you?"

Shrugging, she shook her head. "I've never thought so. I most certainly don't think of you in a paternal way. And while, granted, you're only a bit younger than my mother, you're only ten years older than me. Not many ten-year-old fathers walking around."

"I am closer to your mother's age than yours," he said. "She and I share a generation."

"You really think our age difference is the problem?"

Shaking his head, Martin ran a hand through the thick dark hair she'd had her fingers in just a few nights before. "I think it's part of the problem," he told her. "You put a lot more emphasis on career than I do," he said. "Neither one of us need the money."

Her divorce settlement had been far too generous in her opinion, but he'd insisted.

"I need to be a person in my own right," she told him. For the hundredth time at least.

His nod seemed more resigned than understanding. He'd never really understood.

But he'd tried. She was sure of that. And that counted for something.

"I love you," she said. It should all come down to that.

"I love you, too, Liv, which is why I can't keep doing this."

She was losing him. That was the reality. So maybe his last gift to her had been a baby to raise on her own.

Maybe not. Maybe Beth wouldn't be pregnant and it was all just part of the difficult process of letting go.

Maybe he was right and they'd made it this difficult by not getting it done right nine years before. By letting it drag on so long when they already knew it didn't work.

"I've found a different purpose, Liv." His words were a death knell. "I've got the sense of anticipation back in my life. I'm not turning out to be exactly who I thought I would be. I'm not a family man. I no longer see myself as a father. Or, rather, I am a father, just not as I'd envisioned. After Lily…that picture of raising a child of my own faded away. But… I'm doing good in the world and it feels right. I'm happy."

She thought she'd been happy, too. Was fairly certain she had been…

"I can't bear the thought of losing you," she said. "I'm listening to what you're saying. It makes sense. I see the logic. And then I think about never being able to call you, or know that you're okay, and…what if one or the other of us gets in an accident? Does the other get to know?"

He shook his head. "That's the point," he told her. "We need to cut those ties because, until we do, they'll be pulling us too closely together. So close there isn't enough room left for either one of us to have a partner in our lives."

"You date." She didn't. With her career, her volunteer work, her friends, her love for him, she'd just had no desire…and had told herself she was all grown up and healthy because even though she didn't date, she was able to live with the fact that he did.

"Not seriously. Not in any kind of committed way. How can I? When I know that if you called, I'd likely be unfaithful?"

"But…what about the stocks we still share that we didn't want to sell because they'll be worth more if we hold on to them?" She was grasping.

"Our lawyers can handle any communication or paperwork in the event we decide to sell," he told her.

Originally everything had been set up that way. Until one or the other of them—she couldn't honestly remember who at the moment—had suggested that it was just as easy for them to talk to each other than to communicate through lawyers.

He was so sure. And had ten years' worth of perspective on her.

He had to go. She had to tell him goodbye. But she just stood there and stared at him, doing her best not to cry. Succeeding. For the moment.

As long as she held on to the moment, just stood there, the next moment wouldn't come.

Except that it did. Martin took a step closer. He was going to give her a final, parting hug. She saw it coming. Shook her head. Stepped back.

His hands dropped to his sides, and he cocked his head and reached out again, to touch a lock of her hair, running his fingers down its length, before settling it behind her shoulder. When he sighed, her heart leaped with hope.

"Do you honestly want to try again?" he asked.

Olivia noted that she wasn't jumping for joy.

Instead, she was thinking back to the last months of their marriage, to the things they'd fought about, her dedication to her classes, his need to do more than just hang around LA. He was a doer. One man with the energy of three who bored easily.

She remembered how just being with him had

drained her emotionally—because she'd never been what he'd needed.

She remembered realizing that, while she was in love with him, he hadn't really been what she needed, either.

She still wanted him in her life. To know she could spend a night in his arms. That she could call him if she needed his opinion. That he'd call her if he wanted hers, or to share some news with her.

She wanted what they had. But they weren't good together.

And he was right—maintaining their status quo was preventing both of them from finding anything more anywhere else. With anyone else.

When she glanced back up at him, she knew he was not only waiting for her answer, but he'd already guessed what it was going to be.

"No," she said.

And she stood there alone as he walked out the door.

Chapter Seven

Martin didn't leave Marie Cove right away. He should have, but he just didn't. He'd never lived in the town. Olivia had chosen to do her residency in the small southern coastal community and had accepted the full-time position she'd been offered afterward. She'd been there six years and he'd never bothered to get to know it.

Why do so when its residents no longer had any bearing on his life?

Olivia had lived in Marie Cove almost three times as long as she'd lived with him, yet he'd never really considered her move there to be permanent. She had friends in LA. Spent a lot of her free time there. The majority of it not with him.

Lily was buried in LA. And Olivia visited their daughter a couple of times a month. At least. She left fresh lilies, and they made him feel closer to her when he'd see them during one of his weekly visits. Lily was someone the two of them shared—even if they visited separately.

As he parked downtown and walked along Main

Street, passing by the upscale pubs that called out to him, then drove past the Oceanfront Hospital Complex that had won her away from LA, he fought back the emotion trying to consume him.

Sometime past nine he ended up down at the beach. Sitting in the sand in the dark, listening to the waves as the cool October night breeze washed over him.

There was no doubt in his mind that he'd done the right thing.

For himself, yes, but for Olivia, too. Maybe more for her. She was thirty-one. A successful pediatrician on staff at a prestigious hospital. She had a slew of friends that she kept safely in a social circle, and she had her mother.

She had no partner. No one to rub her shoulders when she came home at night. To hold her while she cried away the grief from losing a patient. No one to laugh with her over a stupid joke at the dinner table.

She was beautiful and vibrant and sexy, and he had no right to continue to hold her. To stand in the way of her finding another man.

A weight had been lifted from his shoulders that night. He knew the future was going to be brighter because of it.

He sat there, looking out to an ocean he could only see through shadows of glistening moonlight, and let the memories wash over him. Olivia the first day they'd met; he'd been stunned with just a look.

The first time they'd made love. The night she'd announced that she was pregnant.

One time, after an evening of lovemaking, she'd insisted on them making a pizza out of whatever they could find in the refrigerator, only to discover that they didn't own a pizza pan. She'd been so disappointed he'd gotten dressed and headed to a twenty-four-hour big-box store and purchased one for her. Along with proper fixings. He remembered licking some of the sauce off her breasts…

Then he remembered her distended belly as she'd carried their daughter. The baby had been small from the beginning, raising some concern, but not enough to warrant more than a close watch. The first time Lily had kicked hard enough for Martin to feel her, he'd thought he'd found heaven. Knowing his child was inside his wife, moving around, kicking out at him—that was something far greater than anything money could buy. Anything he could do himself. He'd been more humbled that night than he'd been as a kid standing in the free-lunch line at school.

He remembered Lily. Not just her tiny body hooked up to tubes that were bigger than she was, but those eyes…round and dark like her mama's. She'd look right at him, and the wisdom he read in that gaze…

Someone, he couldn't remember who, had once said that Lily was an ancient spirit. He'd scoffed at the time, but the words had hung around him ever since.

At some point, Martin became aware of moisture not far from the corner of his mouth. The trickle of tears that were falling slowly down his cheeks. Though he hadn't cried since his daughter's funeral, he didn't fight the slow release of emotion.

Sometime after the moon had passed from the center of the sky, he arose, brushed himself off and made his way back to his car.

Leaving his past back on that beach.

It had been a hard night, a long time coming.

But he'd said his final goodbye to Olivia.

Martin's last visit served at least one good purpose. It managed to distract Olivia's emotional energy somewhat, to burn up enough massive waves to ease at least a bit of the burden of waiting ten days to find out the status of the rest of her life.

She cried more during that first week than she had since Lily's death. And she worked as much as she had during the first year of her residency. Pouring herself into the neonatologist part of her—the part that helped ease suffering and save lives. Work had always been able to consume her, to take her out of herself and give her rational brain the lead. It had saved her life once.

On Wednesday she had the rescheduled dinner with Christine but didn't mention the split with Martin. It was still too new. Too raw.

She had to process before she put it under scrutiny. Which was why she neglected to tell her mother, as well. Some things were too private to be shared.

Jamie was teaching a couple night classes at the arts college on the outskirts of Marie Cove that fall, coinciding with the nights Christine normally volunteered at the women's center. Since William had come, they'd managed to make it all work. Had childcare arrangements and adjusted their schedules to trade off caring for the baby themselves.

Olivia listened, thought about how having a baby changed you from the inside out. Once you'd held that son or daughter in your arms...

Maternal instincts, the magic air that permeated your world just because your child had entered it—that became life's driving force.

Christine thought her relationship with Olivia would remain the same after the second baby came—thought that their friendship wouldn't change—but Olivia knew differently. Two babies would be so much more time-consuming than one.

Olivia felt lonelier than she'd ever been.

But she tried not to let herself imagine how it might be if she and Christine both had babies to raise. Her own hopes for herself weren't a part of this. She couldn't let them be.

Beth called on Thursday to let Olivia know she hadn't had her period yet. The contact wasn't necessary, hadn't been discussed as part of the plan, but Olivia had given the woman her cell number.

"I hope I'm not making this harder or something. It's just I'd be wondering if it was me and…it seems like this baby is everything to you and I wanted you to know."

Olivia's heart was thudding, her mind in cope mode as she sat down at her desk. Tried to find some bedside manner. "I… Thank you," she said. "Please, call me anytime. I…just… Thank you."

The call only lasted seconds. Olivia welled up as she stared at her phone after they disconnected.

This baby is everything to you. Had she given that impression?

Keeping the embryo alive had been all she could think about. Still all she could think about.

It wasn't like this was her only chance to have a child with a surrogate. There was nothing wrong with her eggs. It wasn't about the choice to have a child. She'd chosen long ago not to do so on her own.

But this one…it had been conceived inside of her, had found life there, out of a night of intense bonding. It already existed.

It wasn't a matter of having a baby. It was a matter of saving her child's life.

So, yes, maybe this meant everything to her. Not because she needed to be a mother, but because she needed her baby to live.

On call that weekend, Olivia slept at the hospital—as

was common—and had another quick call from Beth, telling her there'd still been no sign of menstruation.

"I want this for you," the woman said. "I know we don't know each other, but I can't stop thinking of you. I just want you to know that my family and I…it's pretty much all we're talking about. Even my seven-year-old, who doesn't grasp the whole concept, understands that I'm laying low because I'm trying to have a baby for a woman who can't have one. And my aunt and my sister and Brian… Seems like every time I go to the bathroom they're watching me come out, and smile when I shake my head."

It could have been too much information. Olivia, who'd just come into her office with a tray from the cafeteria, settled back onto the couch perpendicular and down the wall from her desk. She had a view of the ocean and stared out to the distant sea. "I can't thank you enough for this," she said, nonplussed. Moved beyond any words she could find. Being privy to intimate family information was not new to her. She spent her days sharing some of the most intense moments as people fought for the lives of their children, bonding to cope. Giving them everything she had.

She'd never been on the receiving end, though.

"Tell them thank you from me," she added before they hung up. But that didn't in any way cover it. No one at work knew that she'd had the procedure. No one knew she was waiting on a very thin precipice.

And those in her life who did know, Christine and Sylvia, were allowing her space as always. She shared when she was ready. Until then, they let her be.

But just south of LA was an entire family giving their energy into seeing her embryo maintain life. Trembling, she grabbed a pillow off the couch, hugged it to her and cried a little. Then a little more. There were hormones involved, she knew that. Her body had been pregnant for a moment. Hormones would have already kicked in to see that embryo safely to her uterus. To prepare her uterus.

But the tears weren't just hormonal.

How could you want something, need it, so badly you couldn't breathe, when you'd thought not having it was what you'd wanted?

There was no room in her life for a baby. She had no idea how to be a single mother. Her condo didn't have a playground, or any place for kids to run about. She worked long hours and was on call every other weekend.

She could be on the brink of living the rest of her life with the possibility of losing another child…

Every emotion within her froze at that thought.

Her soup and sandwich had grown cold, but she ate them. And when, just after ten, she got a stat call to the unit, she presented herself immediately, did her job efficiently and brought Baby V back from the brink of death one more time.

* * *

The pain would pass. Experience had taught him that. Busy schedules were a godsend when one needed distraction from the goings-on inside. And when all else failed, alcohol could take the edge off the immediate stabs of pain. Martin allowed himself a bit of overindulgence for the first week. And when his time was up, forced himself back to his doctor's earlier advice, drinking in moderation, in spite of the excruciating loneliness eating him up inside.

How in the hell did a guy feel lonely when he was surrounded by people who were focused on entertaining him? Listening to him?

Pleasing him?

He'd turned down the couple of offers he'd had over the past days to find forgetfulness in the arms of a beautiful woman. He'd never been keen on using anyone.

Sex had to be open, honest, mutual—or it didn't happen.

It would happen again. He didn't worry about that. He worried about Olivia. Wanted to call, just to make certain she was okay. Sober, he struggled to forget the vulnerable look on her face as they'd said their final goodbyes.

And knew that it was all just part of the process. Knew that he had to stay strong. For both their sakes.

In the past he could appease himself with the

knowledge that she'd call if she had any kind of emergency. Half waited for her to do so, just to talk about their latest breakup one more time if nothing else. To be certain they were doing the right thing.

When a few days had passed and he hadn't heard from her, it had dawned on him that he wasn't going to.

Living without that safety net was proving more difficult than he'd imagined.

Until it hit him—not knowing about Olivia could be a blessing in itself.

The idea was to be free. To move on.

To create a world for himself where he didn't live alone. Travel alone. An existence where he had a partner whose purpose, whose goals, matched his. He'd opened the door.

A new life awaited him.

He just had to welcome the "not knowing" where Olivia was concerned. To figure out how to truly let go. Of her. And of the worry, too.

If he couldn't worry, then he could no longer carry the weight of her grief around with him. He'd carry his own until the day he died. But if he could let Olivia go…if he could quit hurting for her even more than he let himself feel his own pain…

A small bit of relief came with the thought.

He welcomed it. Relief felt good.

Just as the future should.

So he'd cling to it—that small bit of positive emotion. Expand upon it.

Move forward.

Yes, it was that hint of relief that would take him into the future.

He was good to go.

Chapter Eight

Beth Applegate traveled alone to Marie Cove for the pregnancy test that first Thursday in November. She'd called Olivia to invite her to attend her appointment at the Parent Portal with her, but Olivia had a meeting at the hospital and the actual appointment had only been for a blood draw.

However, after having just worked two twelve-hour days, she was off the rest of the day and invited Beth to lunch after the appointment. She and Beth agreed to meet at an upscale restaurant in town with gorgeous ocean views.

She was telling herself that the lunch invitation was to thank Beth for coming forward as she had, especially on a moment's notice, to help Olivia with her problem. Thanking her in person, for the phone calls that had come every two days since the embryo transfer. And...she'd wanted to wait with Beth for the test results, which had been promised within a couple of hours of the blood draw. Drawing on Martin's example, she tried not to think about what those results might show. Tried not to build herself up so high that she'd be irreparably hurt by the resulting fall if the test results were disappointing.

Beth had not yet had her period.

And that didn't mean anything other than that the hormones she'd been given during the transfer process, to help prepare her uterus for implantation, had done their job.

In skinny black jeans, a knitted formfitting purple shirt and black-and-purple short cardigan with the sleeves rolled up, Olivia was the first to show up. And waited for Beth outside the restaurant.

"How'd it go?" she asked as soon as the athletic-looking blonde in colorful leggings and a thigh-length long-sleeved yellow blouse and sandals approached.

"Good," Beth said, smiling as she reached out a hand and squeezed Olivia's. It wasn't a handshake.

The gesture had been more like a hug.

Beth's cheer, her positive nature, seemed to reach even to the ponytail that swung as she walked, and occasionally as she spoke energetically over lunch. Any baby she carried would get a cheerful start on life. Olivia wanted to hug the woman and not let go.

She told Olivia about her classroom filled with twenty-three five-year-olds. About some of the things kids had said that made her laugh. Or taught her about life. She talked about her own seven-year-old. About getting her son through his terrible twos, a phase that he'd apparently carried with him into his threes. And when they both declined dessert but asked for more tea—one decaffeinated, one not— Beth finally quieted.

"My babbling isn't helping, is it?" she asked, her ponytail completely still as she glanced at Olivia across from her.

Olivia smiled, a real smile. "To the contrary," she said. "You're giving me a vivid picture of a lovely life." A life that could be her baby's first exposure. Studies had proven that fetuses took in voices and sounds around them, were affected by a mother's emotions, as they grew in the womb.

"I think it's a great thing you're doing," Beth said then, leaning forward. "Most women, myself included, would probably have opted just to take the pill if they suspected the possibility of an unplanned pregnancy. And with you not being able to carry the child yourself, if the pregnancy did occur, you've got even more reason to just ensure that there'd be no chance of a living embryo."

The cranberry and walnut salad Olivia had had for lunch sat like rocks in her stomach; she struggled to loosen her muscles enough to draw air into her lungs. She could do this.

Hoping the tight expression on her face resembled a smile, she gave the best response she could master. A nod.

"I was thinking maybe we could talk about plans... in the event that the test comes back positive," Beth continued, seemingly undeterred. "I'm assuming you'll want to be at all my doctor's appointments and such, but I'd be happy to make myself available other times, too, so that the baby can get to know your voice. My family has already offered to have you over to share dinners with us, or movie night—we do that every Friday night, with pizza—you know, so you're part of the baby's first environment…"

Lips trembling, Olivia nodded again. "Can we, um, wait until we know?" she asked softly. She didn't want to tamp down one iota of Beth's outgoing enthusiasm. She just couldn't…plan yet.

Didn't know if she had anything to plan for.

"I…don't…" She bowed her head briefly. "I just want you to know that I don't engage in unprotected sex. As a general rule. Never actually. Except this once. I'm generally so careful."

She owed Beth Applegate nothing but money— with a load of gratitude thrown in—but she suddenly wanted Beth to know her. To know that the embryo she was trying to carry wasn't the result of an irresponsible person out for a good time. That Beth's family wasn't dedicating themselves to something in vain. That that embryo was special.

"The father—"

Beth shook her head. "You don't need to do this," she interrupted. "I'm not here to judge. I don't need to know…"

"He's my ex-husband," Olivia explained. "It was

a night of recklessness, of trying to hold on to something long gone. It was stupid and reckless, but it wasn't with just any guy."

Her mouth open, Beth stared at her. And then asked, "Does he know?" She glanced around, as though she'd find Martin sitting at a table close by. Ready to swoop in.

Olivia took a sip of tea. Felt another pang of the guilt that had been plaguing her for not telling Martin what she'd done before they'd said their final goodbyes. Shook her head. "If there's no pregnancy, there's no…" She broke off, shaking her head again.

It all sounded so sordid. So dramatic. When her life, in reality, was lived in a well of practicality.

"We've been divorced nine years," she blurted. And then, before Beth could respond, found herself saying even more. "We…lost a baby…" She, whose own mother and best friend knew better than to ask for confidences from her, was spilling her insides out to a virtual stranger.

But how could you call a woman who'd allowed you to put your embryo inside her—a stranger? Even if the implantation hadn't been successful…just the fact that Beth had allowed it…

A phone rang nearby. She almost tipped over her tea glass. Was shaking visibly, and clasped her hands in her lap. Two hours had passed. She'd eaten. Done her job.

How much longer could this waiting go on?

"You had a miscarriage?" Beth's words brought her away from the fact that they could hear at any moment whether or not her baby had survived the first critical stage of her attempt to save its life.

She shook her head. Thought of Lily. And was strangely calmed. Sad, yes, as always. But calmed, too. In a way she'd never known before. It was like the air coming off the ocean and through the window suspended her there in a cottony wave. She could still feel the booth, hear the mumbles of other conversations, the sounds of silverware and activity. She was fully cognizant. But…held, too.

"She was born prematurely, but was fully viable. Her name was Lily," she shared, and even smiled. Her sweet little Lily of the valley. Born in a valley she didn't live long enough to know. "She lived four months…" And that was as far as she could go.

"You said you've been divorced nine years?"

"Yeah." Not an easy topic, but more manageable.

"So you must have been a kid when you had her…"

"Twenty-one." Ten years had passed since she'd seen Lily. Held her. So hard to believe.

The warm compassion that seemed to encapsulate Beth's face wrapped over Olivia even as she shied away from it. She wasn't the victim of the tragedy here. Lily had been.

"Well, I—"

Whatever Beth had been about to say was cut off as her phone rang.

Eyes suddenly wide, alarmed, she glanced at Olivia, as though waiting for her permission to answer.

"It's okay." This time it was Olivia reaching out to touch. With a squeeze of Beth's hand on the table she said, "Answer it. Either way, it's okay."

Either way. She'd done everything she could do...

And felt helpless. Weak. And so, so, so scared...

"This is Beth." Wasn't sure if Beth had said "hello" first or not.

"Uh-huh..." She was looking at the table.

Beth turned in the booth, facing the room instead of Olivia. "Yes." And then swung back, glancing toward the ocean. "Okay."

One thing was clear: Beth was looking anywhere but at Olivia.

Olivia needed her gaze. Had to know if she'd saved her baby's life. Or at least given the embryo a chance to grow into a healthy fetus.

"Right." The side view she had of Beth's face gave her nothing. A straight face. Seemingly focused.

Because she was trying to figure out how to break bad news?

Or because there was important information to take in? Details of more to come?

"Okay."

What was she agreeing to? Was it Christine on the line? Telling her to have Olivia call her?

She didn't need to be coddled. She needed to *know*.

"I will." What? Take care of herself? Because she was pregnant? Or because that was a common way to say goodbye? Or was she agreeing to pass on information to Olivia? Commiseration, maybe?

Sick to her stomach and clutching the wooden booth so hard she was bruising her fingertips, Olivia forced herself to breathe. Tried to remember that no matter what, she'd handle it.

If there was no baby, there wasn't. She'd done all she could.

She wouldn't have to worry about her life being turned upside down. Wouldn't have to worry about anything.

"Okay, thank you."

She'd have an absolutely empty gaping hole of a life...

"Bye."

Beth looked at her and all Olivia could see were the tears in her eyes. And then the hand sliding across the table. She met it halfway. Held on. Lest she be forever lost in that big black hole of a life.

"It's positive, Olivia. *We* are."

She wasn't sure she'd heard the words correctly. Thought maybe she'd needed them so badly she'd imagined them. Then realized she'd seen Beth's lips move.

"We are?" she repeated, just to be sure.

Beth's nod was short and swift. Vigorous. With her free hand she wiped her tears and then placed it atop the hand that was holding Olivia's. "The test was positive. We're pregnant!"

We're pregnant!

We're...

Oh my God!

The test was positive. Beth was carrying her embryo.

Which meant...

Olivia was going to have a baby!

There was absolutely no reason for Martin to be standing at the opened door of the washing machine Thursday afternoon, cramming in the comforter from his bed. The thing was relatively new—his housekeeper cleaned it regularly, but apparently regularly wasn't every week when she did the sheets.

Olivia's scent on the damned thing was driving him wild. Night after night, he'd climb into bed telling himself he'd had a great day. That he was doing better. He'd look back on all of the hours he'd been gainfully engaged without thinking of her at all. Each day contained something enjoyable. He'd recount it as he lay in the dark.

And he still wasn't sleeping well.

He'd finally figured it out while sitting in his office at Fishnet headquarters that afternoon. The office had just been cleaned and the slightly antiseptic scent had reminded him of his mother. Of the run-down, tiny home she'd insisted on keeping spotless. Of the Saturdays she'd made him clean the bathroom. They'd always have chocolate ice cream afterward.

And it reminded him of something he'd learned in college—scent elicited the Proust effect, reliving experiences through experiencing stimuli.

He'd wrapped up his last couple of appointments, loaded up his briefcase with work he could tackle at home and driven straight to his condo. Inside he'd barely dropped his keys on the table by the door before heading straight to the master bedroom suite, taking his nose straight to the comforter.

Five minutes later there he was, stuffing it into the washer. He'd checked the tag. Knew the thing was machine washable. He just wasn't sure how he could be certain that every little epithelial cell Olivia might have left behind would be removed. He could take it to the cleaners. Or call and have it picked up.

He didn't want to wait.

While he shoved and pondered, his phone rang. Of course.

He only gave that particular cell number out to people he'd want to speak with during nonbusiness hours.

"Martin?" An uncomfortable jolt passed through him. And stuck around, too.

"Olivia?" It was good to hear her voice.

To know she was…there.

"What's up?" He tried to keep his tone casual, but the fact that she was calling meant things were anything but.

"I need to see you."

Glancing at the comforter that may or may not be on his bed that night, he took a moment. Feeling a bit better, knowing that she was struggling, too, he figured he was going to have to be strong for both of them.

"We said we aren't going to do this anymore," he reminded her gently. But would one more time hurt? Just to ease the transition?

"This isn't about us." She sounded different. Olivia, and yet not. Her tone… He couldn't place it. "At least, not directly," she added.

She is getting married. Where the thought came from he didn't know, but the thesis fit. She'd been seeing someone—as she'd been completely free to do, as he'd done many times over the nine years since their divorce, he quickly reminded himself.

That last night together, she'd been different then, too. More the Olivia he'd known in the beginning.

She'd been saying goodbye.

It fit. All the pieces coming together. She'd been struggling, feeling guilty, sad at losing him, but knowing they had to let go.

What must she have thought when he'd told her

he wanted to look for a partner? Knowing she'd already found one…

With a one-handed shove he got the comforter in the washer and slammed the door.

"Martin?"

"Yeah."

"Can we set a time?"

He didn't want to look her in the eye when she told him she'd met someone else. Probably someone years younger than him. Someone who was at the same stage of life as her. Filled with drive to build a career that would carve craters in the heart. Craters only love could fill.

Except that in Liv's case, they'd be building the careers simultaneously, sharing the road. She deserved to have that partner.

"Can we do this over the phone?" he asked, not wanting her to see his expression when she delivered the news. He'd smile. He'd wish her well.

But she always saw through him.

That had been part of their problem. She'd known he wasn't happy even when he'd told her he was fine.

"No. It's important, Martin. I wouldn't ask otherwise."

He got that. But…they were done. Out of each other's lives. No more needing to know. No more reason for her to linger in the back of his mind. He was no longer her protector.

If he'd ever been.

Olivia had always been pretty self-sufficient. Capable of taking care of herself. It was him who'd needed to occupy the protector role.

Something her youth had probably brought out in him.

"Do you trust me to know you well?"

"Of course."

"And to have your back?" she asked.

They weren't doing that anymore. That was the point. But… "Of course."

"Then trust me when I say that you'd want me to be making this phone call and for us to talk in person."

Wow.

He didn't know what to make of that.

Wasn't sure how it played with the theory.

"I've got a couple of hours," he told her, more if he needed it, he determined, thinking ahead to the dinner plans that could be rescheduled. Dinner with his college buddy Danny, who had a wife he adored and a kid heading off to college. One who'd only met Olivia once and teased him about the fact that she hadn't been old enough to legally drink champagne at their wedding. After which Danny had apologized and asked Martin if he was sure about what he was doing by starting a family with a younger woman. The same guy who'd been there a couple of years later when he'd been drinking his way through the death of his daughter and the breakup of said marriage…

"You want me to meet you halfway?" he asked. There was a place in Mission Viejo where they'd met up several times. An upscale, though privately owned, hotel on the beach. It had a nice second-story bar that overlooked the ocean.

"I'm actually already in LA. I was hoping we could meet at your place."

His place? He looked around. Left the stuffed washing machine just as it was. Paced a circle in the kitchen. Came up with no reason he wanted to give her for not wanting her in his home.

"Fine," he said. "I'm here now."

"So am I."

As she said the words the doorbell rang. He'd forgotten to take her name off the list with the doorman. To change his access code.

Or, now that he thought about it, take back her key.

Chapter Nine

He'd obviously just come home from work. Olivia recognized the tie Martin was wearing with his white dress shirt as he opened the door. It was one hundred percent silk and she'd bought it for him for Christmas. What did it mean that he still had it?

And wore it.

Could mean that he didn't remember where he got it, but liked it.

"I'm sorry to barge in on you like this…" With him still in his perfectly polished wing tips and creased black pants with the handmade leather belt, she felt…underdone. Wished she'd stopped home to change before she'd made the trip to LA.

She hadn't been thinking about clothes, to say the least. Mostly her thoughts were all over the place. Not staying long in any one place. Flitting from Beth's words when she hung up the phone, to crib styles, back to future clinic appointment details and over to grandma names for her mother. Shying away from anything that might put a pall on the joy.

Like the fact that the baby's father would not be happy with her news.

"What's up?" There was a lot more concern in his voice than when he'd asked the same question just moments ago. Once she was inside, he slid his hands deep into his pockets, as though caging them there.

Because they wouldn't caress her ever again.

She still hadn't found a way to get to the reality of that one. To accept it.

And now, even if they went their separate ways, she would still have a lifelong connection to him. A little thrill swept through her. And relief did, too.

She didn't have to believe she was never, ever going to see him again.

But she was getting ahead of herself.

"Can we sit down?" she asked. Thinking of him—he should be sitting when she broke her news—but thinking of herself, as well. Her wobbly knees felt as though they could give out any moment.

He led the way to the formal living room—a sunken space that was furnished with large, expensive dark couches that she found too big to be comfortable. She perched on the raised marble hearth in front of the fireplace.

She was going to have a baby! *They* were going to have a baby!

And so much could go wrong before the child even got there. Just because the implantation was successful didn't guarantee that Beth wouldn't miscarry.

Or that something wouldn't go wrong further into the pregnancy.

For a blip there, as she watched Martin settle into a chair that matched the couch and raise his ankle up to rest across the opposite knee, she had second thoughts about telling him. Maybe she should wait.

Just until they'd passed the critical three-month mark at least. A lot of people waited until after the first trimester before announcing baby news.

"Whatever it is, just tell me, Liv. Or maybe I can help. You're getting married, right?"

"What?" Openmouthed she stared at him. "What?" she asked again, frowning.

"I assumed that's what you've come to tell me. That you've been involved with someone and you're getting married."

"We just had the most incredible sex ever thirteen days ago and you think I'm getting married to someone else?" She wasn't sure whether to just stay shocked, or to get pissed, too. "What do you take me for?"

Brows raised, he kind of cocked his head. Half shrugged. The foot dangling over his knee was tapping air in beat with the thumb he was tapping against his thigh.

"Seriously, Martin. You think I'd be unfaithful to a man I was planning to marry?"

It mattered not at all in the scheme of things. And she couldn't let it go. Couldn't get herself back on track. All she'd done, seemed like every second since they'd made love, was think about that night.

Deal with the consequences.

And he thought of it as a roll in the hay? A premarital fling?

"Say something." Her tone wasn't all that kind, but she didn't raise her voice. But then, Olivia pretty much never raised her voice. She was more the "kill them with silence" type.

"You were...different...that night," he said. Which was no answer at all.

"Different?"

"More like..." He shrugged again, meeting her gaze and looking away, several times, clearly uncomfortable. It was a new thing, Martin seeming a bit like a kid to her. She filed the impression away in case she ever had a chance to give it a moment.

"Like what?"

"You'd had a bit to drink."

"So had you."

"You want the truth?"

"Have I ever not wanted the truth?" She could play his game as long as he kept dishing it out. He'd insulted the hell out of her and she didn't deserve that.

He'd cheapened what to her had been an almost spiritual bonding—a night that had completely changed her life. She truly wasn't sure what to make of that.

Wasn't sure if she even wanted to tell him about the consequences of that night, after what he'd said.

"You were more like the woman I married," he told her. "Open. Uninhibited. Hungry."

Oh. Well. He'd noticed that the night had been good, too, then, she translated.

"I thought you were saying goodbye."

She stared. Leaning a bit forward, toward him. Was that why he'd said they couldn't see each other anymore?

"So all that stuff about wanting a partner, about needing to move on—that wasn't true?" she asked. "You were just giving me what you somehow thought I wanted?"

Was the world ever going to right itself?

His vigorous nod, and then shake of his head, just confused her more. "I don't deny that I'd try to give you what you want or need, Liv. I think that's been proven out multiple times over the past ten years. But everything I said was most definitely true. I meant every word, so if you're here to revisit that situation, I'm sorry, Liv, but I'm not changing my mind. Not even for you."

Her mind quieted. Her emotions gathered into a hard ball and settled in her stomach.

Not even for you. Silly, really, considering they were divorced and had recently said a permanent goodbye, but she'd never thought she'd hear those words from Martin. He'd once told her that, no matter what, she'd always hold a special place in his heart.

She'd believed him.

Funny how the older you got, the more you realized that nothing was forever. Every*thing* changed. Every*one* changed. With enough time.

"I'm not here to revisit that situation," she said quietly when she was ready to speak. Even if, in some small part of her, she'd held out hope that the baby might change the new rules implemented between the two of them, she no longer felt that way.

He'd effectively quashed all hope in that one sentence.

Had changed everything between them, effective forever, with those four words.

Because no matter what, she'd never close herself off to changing her mind for him.

Martin didn't like the way the visit was going. Didn't like not knowing what was going on. Didn't like feeling powerless.

Didn't like the way Olivia was suddenly looking at him. Like they were strangers. He wasn't sure he'd ever even seen the invisible shield that seemed to come down over her pupils as he met her gaze. He couldn't read her. It was like looking at blank orbs of color.

What the hell…?

He sat forward, elbows on his knees, hands clasped between them. Facing her. He had to fix this. To help her see that moving forward was best for both of them.

Liv was the smartest person he'd ever known. And had always been open to seeing both sides in any situation. Their problems didn't stem from either of them refusing to see the other points of view but from seeing both and knowing that they didn't fit. Or coexist.

So how did he fix this?

When no answer came to him, he knew he had to slow down. That he needed more information.

"Why did you need to speak to me?" His question filled with all of the caring he'd ever felt for her, he willed her to meet his gaze. For real.

For a second there, he thought he'd been successful. That he'd reached her. He saw a shadow, then maybe a glint, in her eyes, but it was gone too quickly for him to be able to successfully decipher it.

"I came to tell you that there were consequences from that night," she said, sounding like she was giving test results to a patient. At least he assumed that's what he was hearing. She'd certainly never talked to him like that before. As though she was on the outside looking in at him.

"Consequences?" He frowned. "What does that mean? Did you get some kind of infection or something? Because I can guarantee you, I'm completely clean and—"

"Oh my God, Martin! Shut up!" She didn't raise her voice, but he felt slapped. Her tone… If she hadn't been done with him before, it was becoming pretty damn clear that she now was.

She glanced down for a few seconds, then back up. "I apologize," she said, her arms wrapped around her middle like she was cold. He didn't dare offer her the afghan off the couch.

"I got pregnant, Martin. I got pregnant. If you recall, we didn't use protection. I was ovulating. And I got pregnant."

His entire system shut down. Froze. If he had thoughts, he wasn't aware of them. And then he was. Aware that she was sitting there. Her shirt was purple and hugged her beautiful breasts. The cardigan he could do without. His shoes had a smudge on them. Her hair was falling out of its bun, a few tendrils on each side. She didn't usually like that. He did.

Her lips might have moved. He didn't hear anything.

Except a suddenly loud and continuous replay of her voice from a moment before. *I got pregnant, Martin. I got pregnant. I got pregnant, Martin. I got pregnant.*

"You're pregnant." He coughed as he pushed the words through a throat gone dangerously dry. He wanted to glance at her stomach.

Didn't. Couldn't.

Rooted to the edge of his chair, he couldn't do much of anything. Couldn't get through the moment, so he couldn't get past it.

Olivia couldn't bring a pregnancy successfully to term.

How in the hell…?

He was forty-one years old. Had left behind thoughts of being a father. Except to Lily. He was the dad who visited his only child's grave every week and talked things out. He'd be pushing fifty by the time a kid born in nine months would be ready to play serious sports. Most of the dads at softball practice would be younger than him. More agile. More… whatever. He was closer to the empty nest stage of life. Had entered it early, really, when Lily died, and his marriage had gone to the grave right along with her…

"*I'm* actually not pregnant anymore…" She drew the words out. He heard the emphasis on the first word, but attached no significance to it.

Instead, feeling like his head was encased in cotton, like there were little black bugs running beneath his skin, he stared at her.

"You had an abortion?" He didn't judge. Or blame. His question was soft. Caring.

And he had to hold back tears.

Oh God. And where had he been when she'd

needed him? Off telling her that they were never going to see each other again...

"That's why you texted and asked me to call..." He was catching up to some parts of it.

She nodded. And then said, "I didn't have an abortion."

"You lost the baby." He supposed that was for the best. And good that it had happened that quickly.

And needed a moment to grieve, too, before he could be there for her. Not because he was in any way looking to become a father at forty-one, but because he and Liv had never really had a chance.

And the pain just kept on coming...

"I'm...not doing this very well," she said, wringing her hands. "I'm sorry, Martin, I'm just having a really hard time here."

He started to tell her she had no reason to apologize, wanted to go to her, take her in his arms and never let her go, but she held up her hand.

"Let me finish," she said. And then didn't do it. Licking her lips, she glanced at him.

He looked at those wetted lips and wanted to kiss her. To show her that there was good between them, too. To make the horrible feeling permeating the room go away.

"When I left here on that Saturday, I went straight to Christine to get a morning-after pill."

He'd heard of it, of course, but wasn't at all familiar with something that was, from what he'd heard, used more often by young people, college kids. A solution that hadn't been around when he'd been in college. Or sleeping with multiple partners.

"But I couldn't take it," she said, and he cursed a fate that gave Olivia a body that made things so difficult for her.

"Because it would mess with your system?" he asked, calming a bit as she talked, knowing that his job was to be there for her. To help her through. That's why she'd come to him. Because he was the only one who'd understand.

She shook her head, and he was confused again. "Because I just couldn't. If I'd ovulated, chances were the embryo was already in the process of forming," she said. "Taking that pill would kill it."

He nodded, though he thought she was splitting hairs, being far harder on herself than she needed to be. Which had been a problem with them in the past, too.

After Lily's death, the woman he'd fallen in love with had disappeared, taken over by someone who blamed herself for something that was absolutely not any fault of hers. She'd been a victim of her malfunctioning uterus as much as their daughter had, but she'd never accepted as much. She'd been so certain she could see both sides—but then, if you couldn't see what you weren't seeing, how would you know?

But...wait... She hadn't taken the pill...and she hadn't had an abortion. She wasn't pregnant.

"No way…after Lily…there was just no way I could kill another life that had formed inside me."

He got that. Completely. "So you had an early miscarriage," he guessed again, a bit dizzy with the circles, but determined to stick with her.

She was… Olivia. He couldn't *not* sit with her through this.

"I had an embryo transfer, Martin."

"A what now?" Squinting, he stared at her as though, maybe, she was a mirage. That he'd had more than the one beer at lunch. Or was having one hell of a sick nightmare and would wake up any second.

With no comforter on his bed.

"I had the embryo removed from my womb at the blastocyst stage, before uterine implantation, and had it implanted in a surrogate. We found out today that the procedure was successful."

He nodded, his brain a bit behind on putting meaning to the words. He got the word *successful*, though.

It came through loud and clear.

"What are you telling me?"

"I'm going to have a baby." She said it so calmly. So matter-of-factly. He could be forgiven for thinking she was telling him she was accepting a new position at the hospital. Or buying a new car.

Then his heart started to thud. "You can't have a baby, Liv. You know what will happen…"

"I'm not carrying it in my body," she said, and

he knew what she was saying. He just had no idea in hell what he was supposed to do. To say. To feel.

"There's a woman out there, this surrogate, who is, at this moment, pregnant with our baby." He had to get it out there. Just for the record.

"Yes." She smiled, almost apologetically. And he knew what was different about her.

She was wearing the glow of motherhood again.

It looked good on her. Fit.

And left him sitting there looking not good. Feeling bad.

Olivia was alive again. More like the wife he'd adored. The pregnancy had given her a new lease on life.

And he felt…upset.

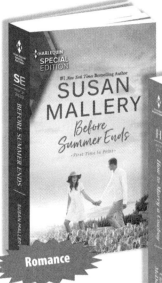

LOYAL READER
FREE BOOKS VOUCHER

HARLEQUIN Reader Service —**Here's how it works:**

▼ If offer card is missing write to: Harlequin Reader Service, P.O. Box 1341, Buffalo, NY 14240-8531 or visit www.ReaderService.com ▼

BUSINESS REPLY MAIL
FIRST-CLASS MAIL   PERMIT NO. 717   BUFFALO, NY

POSTAGE WILL BE PAID BY ADDRESSEE

HARLEQUIN READER SERVICE
PO BOX 1341
BUFFALO NY 14240-8571

NO POSTAGE
NECESSARY
IF MAILED
IN THE
UNITED STATES

Chapter Ten

"I should have had a say in this." Martin wasn't proud of the words. Feeling ripped open, helpless, with all control of his life stripped away from him, he stared at his ex-wife sitting over there, happy, reminding him of a kid at Christmas. She was young. Ready to take on life. He was smack-dab in middle age. Hanging out with friends whose kids were heading off to college.

Needing three showerheads to deal with muscles that had taken up complaining as a way of life.

And it would only get worse as the kid grew. He'd be fifty when the kid was nine. Hell, he was only a few years younger than Olivia's mother, the baby's grandmother.

He was completely unsure of himself as a father to a living child...

"I texted and asked you to call." Her words came softly. Almost tentatively. He heard guilt and part of him wanted to cash in on it. Except there was no value in doing so.

And no reason, either. He wasn't blaming her for

her choice. He was railing against a fate that had irrevocably changed his life without a heads-up. Or any say. He couldn't even wrap his head around the future ramifications.

As a provider, he'd be right there.

"You said it wasn't an emergency," he said back, equally soft. And probably with some guilt attached. He'd been as remiss as she had the night of the greatest sex he'd had since…her. In the early days. Which had been the best he'd ever had, period.

He could have stopped things after she'd unexpectedly slid home. Could have pulled out and applied a condom, or even put one on beforehand.

She was nodding.

Leaning over, elbows still on his knees, staring at the floor, he glanced over at her. "It's a moot point."

"Because it's done. Too late to do it differently."

"Because there's no way I would have ever asked you to kill an embryo," he said. "I wouldn't even have suggested doing so, though I'd have supported your choice, your right to the choice, either way."

"I figured…if there wasn't a viable embryo, or if implantation was unsuccessful, there was no reason to bother you with it."

No reason to bother him with it?

The words hung there. She'd been scared to death of the consequences resulting from an action for which he was equally culpable, and she'd felt like he'd given her no reason to "bother" him with it. They'd become that far removed from each other.

He'd succeeded in creating the chasm between them he needed.

And, after doing so, was facing a situation that would bind them together for life.

"If the choice had been yours, me aside, what would you have done?"

It wasn't a question he wanted to ask himself. Her big brown eyes implored him, communicating some deeper need, whether or not she'd intended to. Whether or not the need was there.

He felt the pull of her. Fought and welcomed it at the same time. This was exactly the situation he'd tried so hard to eradicate—this constant back and forth with her.

They weren't right for each other, but he couldn't get them out of each other's lives, either.

She wasn't asking about their lives, though. She was asking about the new life just beginning to form out there somewhere, in the body of a stranger.

A new life.

A child.

Their child.

"If I'd been offered the chance of a pill to prevent the pregnancy, I'd have taken it," he said. And the silence that fell demanded that he finish. "If I'd been told the circumstances as you've presented them, the chance of a live embryo already having formed, with everything we went through with Lily, how hard we all fought…" He glanced up at her, his head hurting, his throat dry. "I would have had to try to save the embryo."

Tears flooded her eyes. She didn't get up and move closer to him. Didn't speak. And he felt as though he'd been put in a straitjacket with the bindings growing tighter by the second.

"I'll be in my fifties before the child is even out of elementary school." He wasn't sure how that mattered, how any of it played out. But it didn't sound good.

"I'm not asking, or even expecting, you to take this on, Martin." Olivia's nurturing tone got his attention. "I knew when I made the choice that if it was successful I was signing up for single motherhood."

What was she saying? Had she forgotten who he was? "There is no way on earth I'm walking away from this," he told her.

"You aren't walking back in, either."

Not sure if she'd been making an observation or a definitive statement, he shook his head. "Truth be told, I have no idea what I'm doing. Struggling, that's what I'm doing." He glanced at her, his gaze serious and solid. "But I am not walking away. I will be financially responsible for our child starting now. I want to be involved in the process, however much I can be. See…this is what I mean. I have no idea what having a child by surrogacy even entails, in terms of the actual process. I'm assuming there were legalities worked out before the implantation took place."

For a second, he felt a bit like himself, as his brain kicked in and thought of the practical conditions of the moment they were in. He listened as Olivia explained the process, the documents that had been signed. Looked at them on his phone as Olivia sent copies of them from her cell to his. He asked questions. About the embryo transfer process. About Beth and her family.

"I need to meet her. Obviously, since you're going to be in touch with her, visiting with her, it would be appropriate for me to be involved."

Olivia's frown was swift and clear.

"I have rights, too," he said. Obligations, more like it. He knew he was a good, responsible man.

"I'm not arguing that," she told him, still sitting on that hard marble, her hands stuffed between her lower thighs, as though they were holding them tightly. "But we need to talk about all of this…"

"That's what we're doing. Talking."

"You're acting like we're in this together. As a couple."

"That's how we made a child," he said. "Together. As a couple."

"A couple for a night, not a lifetime."

He didn't know what to say to that. Wasn't ready to go down that road.

"Just to be clear, I'm not looking for us to get back

together," she told him before he could even wrap his mind around where they went next. They'd made a baby together. They had to provide for it together. That's what he knew. Where he sat.

"A week ago you were at my house, saying we were never going to see each other again," she reminded him. And those bindings tightened another notch as he imagined how that visit must have affected her, him saying that while she was waiting to see if her embryo had survived implantation. She hadn't given him a clue how she'd been suffering.

And that bothered him, too.

"I didn't know a week ago that we possibly had a child on the way," he said, for want of anything better.

Olivia stood. She didn't come closer, just stood. Either her butt was going to sleep on the marble, the cold and discomfort getting to her, or she was telling him quite clearly that she wasn't taking any argument from him sitting down.

"The reasons you gave were valid," she told him. "We don't fit. We're in two different places in our lives. Our goals, but even more important, our needs, are different. A baby doesn't change any of that. And couples trying to make it work because of a child are clichéd disasters for a reason. It doesn't work."

For the first time since the conversation had started, he regained a semblance of being somewhat in control of his life. He knew a hint of relief. Because she was letting him off the hook. But he was still going to hold on to the responsibility. For no reason he could decipher at the moment. Just good to be holding on.

He studied her as she moved to the sofa. Settled into the corner, slipping off her flats, to bring her legs up, her feet tucked up as she used to do when she watched television.

"I wasn't going to propose," he said. But only because he hadn't gotten that far. He probably would have reached that point. If she'd given him another hour or so. It was the right thing to do. "But I don't think we should take remarriage off the table, either."

She shook her head. "I can't leave it there, Martin. I've got a life to build here and I need it on a solid foundation."

"So we'll put it on a shelf…way up high…" He pointed over the top of the entertainment center, to the plant shelf built just below the ceiling. He had no idea why he was pushing her on it. She was right. Marriage wasn't for them.

But it seemed easier to talk about than the rest of it. Easier to tackle.

Which didn't mean a heck of a lot.

He was finding it easier to tackle something that was already doomed—their failed romance—than to come to terms with the idea of a new life entering the world. One with the power to destroy them, as Lily's loss had. He was a good dad to her. Thought of her every day. Visited her regularly. Never forgot. But she took everything he had to give in the dad department.

What did that say about him?

Martin was pretty sure he didn't want to know.

She had to get out of there. The topic at hand was the embryo they'd made, but Martin was making it about them.

"This isn't about us," she said when he seemed to be waiting for a response to his up-high-shelf comment. He was just sitting there, and she honestly had no clue what he was thinking.

She had come into the meeting unsure of him or what his reaction might be. Ten years ago, he'd have been ecstatic. Nine years ago, even. He'd wanted to search for alternative options for starting their family after Lily died. Her refusal to even consider parenting again had been one of the nails in their coffin.

But he was a different man now. With a completely different life.

She'd called Christine on the way from lunch to LA. Christine already knew the test results, but Olivia had needed to share them with her, anyway. Christine had wanted to know all about how Olivia was doing, assuring her the conglomeration of feelings coming at her was completely normal. And she'd warned her against going straight to Martin with her emotions so raw. Warned her that his reaction would almost certainly be vastly different from what it had been ten years before. Warned her to remember how much had changed between them individually, as well.

Still…to have him just be so calm, like it was no big deal…

"This is about the baby," she continued when her previous comment elicited no response. Maybe she should go. She uncurled her legs. She'd called Sylvia on the way to LA, too, to let her know the results. Sylvia had been beside herself joyful to know they were going to have a baby in the family, that she was going to be a grandma. And she warned Olivia about going straight to Martin like he was still her husband. Her partner.

What struck her as she'd hung up was that Sylvia was going to be a grandparent, was ready to be one—ready to babysit, but not have the responsibility of raising a child. Meanwhile, Martin, who was in his forties, as well, just a few years younger, was the parent.

"I just thought you had a right to know what was going on," she said when the silence got too uncomfortable to sit with any longer. "It's not like there's anything for either of us to do at the moment. We need to get through the first trimester first."

"Why?"

"There's a ten to twenty-five percent chance that Beth will miscarry." She was living with the facts right in her face this time. No fairy tales or dreams of some nebulous perfect world.

"That's what they said when you were pregnant with Lily."

She was surprised that he remembered. Surprised that he'd mentioned their daughter right then. Lily's existence, their differences in handling the aftermath, had become an elephant in the room long ago. They'd both loved and lost. Neither of them forgot. They shared the loss. They just hadn't been able to share the grief.

He was probably right to mention her, though. With a new life to think about, they were going to have to work through their past.

"It's about the same with implantation as it is with natural conception. My thought is that our chances might be a tad better than normal in vitro because the embryo formed naturally inside me, but that's only theory. Not in any way backed by scientific information."

He nodded. Just sat there and moved his head, when she needed to move around. Keep busy. Maybe jump up and down for a second or two.

And bury her head, too.

Her embryo had implanted! It was alive. Being nurtured!

And yet so much could go wrong in the next eight and a half months.

"As long as we get to twenty-four weeks, it will

be viable," she said. In extreme cases a baby born earlier than that could live, but quality of life would likely be a major issue if it did.

Martin glanced from the floor to her, his gaze warmer. "You going to be okay with this?"

"Of course."

"It's okay if you aren't," he told her. "After what we went through with Lily…"

She held up a hand. They could acknowledge it, but she couldn't handle a full-length rerun at the moment.

"You weren't a neonatologist back then and it was still hard. I can't imagine, with all you know now, all you see every day…specializing in working with babies that are born with things having gone wrong in the womb. Or at birth…"

He'd hit that nail on the head. "I know," she told him, giving him the first completely natural look that day. Letting him see the tumultuous emotions she was trying to contain. "Believe me, I know. I'm scared to death."

It felt good to be honest.

Most especially because she knew he really understood.

"It's probably going to be overwhelming at times."

"Yeah."

"Will you at least think about calling me when it happens? I failed you in the past, Liv, but this I know

I can do well. I can listen. I can understand. And I can talk you down."

Because he was better able to see the bright side than she'd ever been. She hadn't grown up in a solid cocoon of security. Hadn't had that safe place from which to learn about the world. Though her grandmother had loved her hugely, been good to her, she'd also raised her to see reality, consequences, in everything. She'd failed to protect her own daughter from mistakes and she'd tried to make darn certain she didn't fail Olivia.

She nodded.

"I don't know how to handle this," he said then. "I know I can support you, financially and in other ways, too. I want to be kept apprised every step of the way. I want to be there for you."

Finally.

It was like Martin had just entered the room.

"I want that, too," she said. Though she was being so careful not to build expectations.

"But I don't feel like I'm ready to be a father, Liv. Not anymore. I don't see myself in that role. It's like telling me I have to go back to college and get the degree I've already earned and am no longer qualified to use." He swallowed but didn't look away this time.

She saw a sheen of moisture in his eyes that she hadn't seen in years.

It was almost as though they'd stepped back in time. Good people who cared about one another but were at odds at their core. One ready. One not. Except that their roles had now reversed.

If their fetus grew into a baby, was born into the world, she was completely certain she was going to take up the role of parent with every fiber of her being.

He said he wasn't able to see himself doing that.

"I'm not asking you to be a father." How could words, expressing something she'd already decided, hurt so badly? "As I told you, I went into this knowing full well that I was doing so as a single mother. I had the papers drawn up in my name only. I didn't name you as the father. I'm the only one who signed them. They've been notarized and filed. All legal means were taken to keep you out of it."

He could petition the courts for DNA samples after the baby was born, have his rights instated. But she wasn't going to compel him to do so.

"That's not right, either. I am as much responsible for this as you are."

"A baby needs love, Martin, not a sense of obligation."

He frowned. "What? You think I won't have feelings for the child? That I wouldn't love my own kid?"

He blinked. Sat back.

"It's not the love," he finally said. "Of course I'm going to love it." He shook his head. "I love you, but that didn't make our life together successful. Didn't

mean we were good, or even healthy, at being together. It wasn't for the best."

"I know."

He didn't speak for a long time. She didn't know
what to say. As the silence continued, and minutes
were passing, she figured she should just go. But sat
there, anyway.

Because she couldn't just get up and walk out on
him. And leave him alone like that.

She'd had thirteen days to process. And the whole
time she'd had the possibility that the implantation
wouldn't take—the knowledge that she might have
nothing to deal with.

He'd had an hour to process. And he had a done
deal.

"I'd like my name to be added to the legal agreement." He tapped his fingers on the chair, looking
over at her. "I don't know if that's possible, or how
it works, with the paperwork already being filed. I'll
check with Robert…"

His personal lawyer. A college friend. The man
who'd handled their divorce.

"I think we can just add an amendment," she said.
"There's specific surrogate law so that all parties are
protected. Regardless, I'll have my attorney look into
it. If nothing else, you have the option of completing
a DNA test when the baby is born and those results
will allow you all rights of fatherhood."

"I don't want to wait until then. What if, God forbid, something was to happen to you before then?"

Her chest muscles relaxed, allowing a bit of tension to ease out of her.

Martin might not be husband material. He might not even be father material.

But he was going to have her back.

And the baby's, too.

"I'll call my lawyer in the morning and see what we have to do to get you added to the paperwork." She wasn't opposed to the idea. Just hadn't wanted him to feel pressured, or as though she was forcing something on him. She'd been prepared to go solo.

And felt a tiny stirring of happy inside her. The fetus was alive. If all progressed well, she was going to have a baby! And Martin was going to participate.

He not only wasn't out of her life for good, as she'd feared he would be. To the contrary, it sounded as though he would be in it for good.

She smiled. He stood up.

Her cue to get going, she figured.

With her purse on her shoulder she followed him through the opulent space to his front door, noting that it wasn't at all babyproof.

But then, there was no reason for the baby to ever be there. Martin was taking on responsibility. He wasn't taking on fatherhood.

Not at all sure how that would define itself, she

knew the distinction was important. And one to which she must adhere.

At the door he turned, faced her. She moved toward him naturally to slide into his arms. Not to kiss or get sexual—they didn't always have to be on each other's bones—but until the other night at her place, they'd always hugged goodbye.

His expression changed…went from someone she knew to a stranger. She stepped sideways. He opened the door, and she walked through it.

A rehearsal for their new normal.

Chapter Eleven

Martin went to dinner with Danny. Asked about his friend's kids and paid much closer attention to the answers. He didn't share the news Olivia had handed him that afternoon. Before he went to bed that night he handwrote and signed an addendum to his trust, naming the baby that a woman named Beth was carrying for Olivia Wainwright as his heir, with Olivia as the executor, and texted his attorney to let him know where it was.

On Friday morning, he was already waiting outside his lawyer's office by the time the man arrived. And had put in motion the paperwork necessary to get himself named on the surrogacy agreement, the birth certificate, and to add the baby officially as the heir to his trust, instructing his lawyer to work with Olivia's. The two had worked together on more than one occasion to deal with financial holdings that Martin and Olivia still shared. The rest of that day he spent in his office, losing himself in work and, in doing so, finding himself again.

He'd come up for air, think about Olivia. About

the night they'd spent. About the idea of a new life in the world. Each time, he was driven to do something. To get up and go take care of it. And then would realize there was nothing for him to do but get back to work.

He had a gala that night—an awards banquet he was cosponsoring for professional athletes who were involved with programs for at-risk kids in their communities—and had invited Victoria Allen, the lawyer he'd met two weeks before, to accompany him.

The plan had been to spend some time with her, to see if anything sparked between them, but as hard as he tried, he couldn't focus on her that night. He suspected she realized, hoped she didn't, or that she'd put his preoccupation down to business matters, and dropped her off with a brief good-night kiss at her door.

Olivia had been out of his life for good when he'd issued the invitation.

Now she was bringing his baby into the world.

It wasn't even ten o'clock yet and he thought about stopping for a drink on his way home. Passed on the option. Passed the freeway entrance, too, and was tempted to drive down to Marie Cove. To get things cleared up with Olivia.

Maybe just to see her.

When he realized he was falling back into the trap of putting her first, he decided against that option, as well.

For all he knew she was on call. Or on a date.

Because he really knew very little about her daily life and regular activities. For the sake of his own mental health he'd quit asking.

In the end, he drove around the city for hours, visiting areas where he'd never been, parts of town he frequented regularly, areas he'd been but didn't visit often, including the old neighborhood where he'd grown up. It had been the recipient of a city grant and was now a thriving middle-class area with small but nice houses with lights shining from them, set in the midst of mowed yards with flower beds.

He ended up outside the gate in front of the house he'd lived in when he met Olivia. The house they'd shared. The house with the nursery that Lily had never been home to inhabit. Parked across the street, he looked up to the second-floor window in the distance, visible through the trees that were scattered around the acre of front yard. It was the master suite light.

He'd sold the home to an investor but had heard that it had been purchased again since. He had no idea who lived there now. If they had kids.

As the light upstairs went out, he remembered the night Olivia had told him she was ready to try to start the family he so badly wanted. They'd gone upstairs to bed, and he was nude and ready under the covers, waiting for her to come out of the bathroom, picturing her in the new teddy she'd ordered and had told him had arrived that day.

She'd been in underwear and a bra instead as she'd come running into the room, flipping on a light as she did so. She'd held a little white stick in her hand, and the glow in her eyes, the energy pulsing all around, had been completely captivating. "I took a test and I'm ovulating."

From that second on he'd needed to protect her as fiercely as he'd ever protected anything. Was she comfortable, eating right, sick to her stomach? Could he rub her shoulders or her back? Did she need him to do anything for her? Because she was doing the ultimate for him—she was willing to grow his baby inside her. Something he could never, ever do himself.

He was in awe of her.

In love with her.

Couldn't stand to be away from her.

She wasn't carrying his baby this time around. And didn't seem to need him for anything. As far as he could tell, she was planning to go on with her life as normal until after the first trimester, and then… she was planning to go on with her life without him.

She had to. They'd called it quits.

He still knew it had been the right thing to do.

He just had no idea what the future needed of him. Was greatly bothered by the idea that whatever it was, he might not be asked. If he didn't figure it out on his own, he'd fail in providing it.

If Olivia ever remarried, her new husband would be the likely father to her child. He'd figured that out after she'd left the night before. A man in his early thirties would be more apt to be up for the twenty-year commitment raising a child required. He'd definitely be better able to run for touchdown passes, and probably better at sitting up all night worrying about parties and sex and drugs when the kid was in high school and missed curfew, too.

She hadn't said anything about another man in her life. Ever. But he'd probably made it plain to her multiple times over the years how very much he didn't want to know.

She'd been offended that he'd think she'd slept with him when she was planning to marry another man, but that didn't mean there wasn't another one in her life. Only that she hadn't fully committed to him yet.

Maybe the baby would be the impetus the guy needed to ask. Or a reason for her to ask sooner than she might have done. Nothing said the man had to do the asking.

He was getting morose. The house seemed to have that effect on him—one of the reasons he'd moved out and sold the place.

A car came up behind him, slowing as it passed, and not wanting to make residents suspicious or uncomfortable, he put his luxury SUV in gear and headed on down the road.

Leaving the past behind.

Olivia had just come from an emergency on the unit Saturday—not Baby V, but still one that she'd managed to treat with some measure of success—when her phone rang. The small sleeping room attached to her office, large enough only for the twin bed and small nightstand it held, beckoned, but she grabbed the phone out of her pocket immediately. She was on call.

It wasn't her hospital phone ringing. Reaching into her other pocket, she grabbed her personal cell quickly, as though the ringing would disturb someone. Heart in her throat, she checked to see if Beth was calling. If there'd been some kind of emergency.

When she saw Martin's ID, she knew she had to calm down. It wasn't fair to anyone, not herself, the baby, Beth or any of her patients, for her to overreact to stimuli for the next nine months. Not that her patients were suffering. Or would suffer. When she was with a patient it was like she was a different person. Better than herself. More capable. That sense of superior ability was one of the reasons she loved her job. It was like every time she held another person's life in her hands, she knew she could handle the job.

She had to find a way to bring that same sense of confidence into her personal life. Had to assume that everything was going to be fine. And to know that she only had to deal with bad news if it happened, and when it happened—just as she counseled her families.

Telling and doing were so not at all the same thing.

"Hello?" She answered on the fifth ring, slipping out of her flats. The scrubs would eventually go in the can by the door. A cupboard next to it was filled with clean ones. A lot of hospital personnel handled their own uniforms. She had a service take care of hers.

She wished at the moment that she had someone to take care of the Martin situation for her, too. She couldn't ask him for help in that regard—that would put expectation out there and she'd told him that he was free to be as uninvolved as he wished.

She couldn't really talk any of it over with him, either, for the same reason. But if they didn't talk about who he was going to be in the child's life, or what part he wanted to play, how did she plan her future?

She'd had calls from two lawyers—his and hers—before she'd even arrived at work the previous morning because he'd already taken care of something she'd told him she'd do.

"Is this a bad time?"

After nine on a Saturday night wasn't a good time to hear from your ex who'd just told you he never wanted to see you again and then turned around and relegated remarriage to a shelf.

"I'm at the hospital tonight," she told him, adding, "On call," lest he think she was in the middle of a traumatic emergency. "I'm in my office, ready to lay down and get some sleep." In case a little one went into stress in the middle of the night or was born in the middle of the night needing immediate attention.

"Thank you for getting the papers done so quickly."

All she'd done was sign on her designated lines. The lawyers and Beth and Martin had done the rest.

Her surrogate had called her before signing, though. Beth hadn't been about to sign anything unless Olivia was completely on board. She wasn't going to be a part of Olivia being coerced.

The woman's concern, though misplaced, had been sweet. And had warmed her, in spite of how unnecessary it had been. Beth didn't seem to understand that Olivia was a respected specialist who handled trauma like most people handled groceries. With care. But also regularly and well.

"I need to meet the surrogate. Beth Applegate. And would prefer to have her husband, Brian, present, as well," he said. "I'm told it's within my parental rights, now that I'm being officially added to the paperwork. The lawyers offered to set it up, but I don't want to barge in here. This is your deal."

Like he hadn't barged in with the paperwork? The

pithy response came to her, but she was tired, and knew better than to voice pettiness. She was better than that and he didn't deserve it. Still… "I was going to handle the paperwork, Martin."

His silence made her feel somewhat better.

"I know you had the right to do what you did. But I told you I'd handle it."

"I was trying to help," he said.

In the past, he'd done things the same way: taking over. His experience gave him better perspective. It was true. But experience and perspective weren't all that went into making choices.

"I know." They'd had the discussion more times than she could count over the years. He was who he was. And she was a woman entrusted with lives; she needed to be respected as someone who could take care of things.

"I figured I screwed up ten minutes after I'd set the wheels in motion."

"A phone call would have been nice," she replied.

"Point taken."

She hated how he took control. But loved that he cared. That he was responsible and reliable. That he had her back.

"We spoke on Thursday about my meeting with Beth Applegate, but we got sidetracked. And this is me now not barreling ahead on my own, in case you didn't notice."

"I noticed." Dropping down to the couch, she

curled her feet up beneath her. "Beth called me before she signed the papers yesterday," she told him. "So how do you want to work this? You just want my okay and then have your lawyer set something up with hers?"

"I was hoping you'd set something up and come with me." He sounded almost like a kid, needing assistance, and it dawned on her that he was unsure of himself. And had been on Thursday, as well.

She'd seen him frustrated. Happy. Confident. Grieving…

She couldn't remember ever seeing Martin Wainwright be unsure of himself. And eased up a bit on her defensiveness where he was concerned.

"It's awkward," he said when she didn't immediately respond. "Hi, I'm Martin, thank you for carrying the baby my ex-wife and I created…"

She didn't quite smile, but almost. Scooting down so she was half lying back, she moved her shoulders around until they were comfortable.

"And it's not like we're a couple, doing this together. They know that, right? Since you started out doing it on your own. But now maybe they'll think we're back together and—"

"They don't." She had to put the man out of his misery. Or at least shut him up for a second. "Beth knows the situation." As well as anyone did, she figured.

"I'm glad someone does. Would you mind filling me in?" There was no sarcasm in his tone. He sounded more lost than anything.

"As soon as I figure it out," she told him quietly. She was tired. Had just saved a baby from dying—for the moment. The prognosis on that night's patient wasn't overly good.

Which was where miracles needed to come in.

"What do you expect from me?"

There they were…the expectations… Hers and his hadn't coexisted well before.

"Honestly, Martin? Nothing. I'm not even sure what to expect from myself at the moment. This is all happening so fast, and completely contrary to my life plan. But I have to say, when I let myself picture a crib with a healthy baby in it, in my home… I'm realizing that there's nothing I want more. I didn't think I'd ever get here, that I'd ever want to even try to have a family again. And while I wouldn't ever make the choice to consciously go make one, because I know all of the things that can go wrong and I'd rather live alone for the rest of my life than risk that again, I'm finding that…faced with the possibility of a healthy baby, a child that will grow into a healthy adult… I'm…excited."

His silence didn't feel comfortable.

He hadn't asked about her feelings about the baby.

Expectations. He needed his parameters. Like always.

"I'm not expecting anything from you." She finally got to a place where the truth was okay. "If I never hear from you again, then I don't. I'm making my plans as though I won't."

"Would you rather I back away? That I not be involved?"

If that's what he wanted.

"That's not what I'm saying."

"What *are* you saying?"

"That you can't put this on me. You have to figure out for yourself what your role is, what your parameters are, who you are in this situation." And then she had to amend her great truth. "I guess I do have a couple of expectations. I expect you to figure it out. And to tell me when you do, so I can make room for whatever you decide."

That was it. She felt lighter. Easier.

"Tell me one thing…"

"If I can."

"Do you want me involved?"

She shook her head, even though it was awkward with her position, even though he couldn't see. "No way, Martin. You aren't putting this choice on me."

"Let me rephrase that. If I choose to be involved, beyond the financial obligation for which I'm already fully committed, will that bother you?"

She knew the answer. Tried to decide if giving it to him somehow made her culpable of trying to sway him or wrap him around her little finger, or whatever it was he'd said to her over the years.

Decided that it was a fair question.

"No," she said. "It won't bother me." To the contrary. She welcomed anything he wanted to give to them—her and her embryo. Anything he had for the mother and child.

Not for the woman in her.

He didn't respond and she was reminded of the man who'd been there, but so seemingly absent in his apartment two days before. This was a new side to Martin. A new Martin. One who seemed to need assistance from her. Not just love, or adoration, or sex.

"So…what kind of involvement are you thinking about?"

"None."

Okay, then. That shouldn't hurt her feelings. She'd had no expectations.

"Except to meet the surrogate," she reminded him.

"Right."

"You sure you want to do that?"

"Absolutely."

Which was involvement.

"Maybe we should just take this one situation at a time for now," she suggested, needing to help him. Not because of the baby. But because he was the only man she'd ever loved and she'd always want to help him. He'd just never seemed to need it before.

"Okay. Good. Yeah, that sounds good. So, for now, I should meet Beth and Brian. Are you okay to arrange that? And to be there?"

"Yes."

"Good." He gave her a rundown of his schedule for the next several days. And then told her he'd rearrange anything he could or cancel what he could if he had to.

"I'm sure we can work something out for when you're free," she told him.

"Good." It was the third "good" he'd given her in as many seconds. Or close to it.

"I'll call her tomorrow and get back with you," she said then, knowing their conversation had to end, but not wanting him to be gone from the other end of the line.

"Good. Sounds good."

And that was it. Their baby business was done and he hung up.

But when she went in to lie down for whatever time she'd have, she kept hearing him saying "good." And realized that for the first time in a long time, she wanted more than just good from him. And for their lives, together or not.

Chapter Twelve

Martin worked fourteen hours on Sunday before attending a cocktail party that night to honor a newly elected politician who was supportive of legislation that would give tax breaks to Fishnet's facilities. Since his organization wasn't a school, and wasn't part of the foster care system, but rather held guardianships until their kids turned eighteen or had agreements with the custodial parents, much like a boarding school would, they didn't fit into existing tax break parameters in a lot of areas. He was hoping to see that fixed.

And on Monday, since Olivia had said she'd make the appointment with the Applegates to coincide with his schedule, he was flying to London for a series of meetings there to finalize plans for an exchange student program. And then it was on to Washington to lobby for funding for boarding of at-risk kids. As things currently stood, when underage kids came to Fishnet, because it was a private organization with ample funds, the young adults no longer qualified for welfare or some of the other government assistance programs. He was also meeting with a grant board while he was there and doing a friend a favor and speaking at a gathering of Ivy League techie grads about the dot-com he'd created as a poor college kid barely getting by.

In exchange, his friend was writing a sizable check to Fishnet.

There were dozens of other things on his schedule. A side trip to New York. And to Boston. Dinners. Parties. Financial meetings and meetings with officials to expand Fishnet into three more cities on the east coast. And then back to LA for a movie premiere.

He traveled alone, and yet, other than his time in the air or the few minutes he had in his hotel suites, he didn't have a minute, or a meal, to himself.

His choice. His life fulfilled him. Energized him.

He wasn't ever lonely or bored.

Or if he was, he was too busy to notice.

The week progressed as planned; his meetings were successful. He was using his life to leave the world, particularly the underserved young adults in it, a better place to grow and thrive. He was parenting in the way he could and was good at it.

And he kept waiting for Olivia to call. She'd texted once, to say that the Applegates were free Sunday, a week and a day after they'd talked. True to her word, she'd worked things around his schedule. She'd done what she'd said she'd do.

And nothing more.

Which left him far too much mental space for speculation apparently. The seconds throughout the day where his brain had a moment to itself, he'd think of Olivia, wondering how she was handling the idea of massive change to her life. Was she managing her fears?

He'd see a mother or a baby and be reminded that he had a child coming into the world. And draw a blank after that.

In a taxi one morning he found himself pondering the fact that she wanted the baby—when she'd been so adamantly against even a mention of the possibility all the years since Lily's death. He worried that circumstances, their recklessness, had forced her into something for which she wasn't ready.

She'd make a great mom. He'd always known that. The child would be blessed…

His thoughts were diverted as he arrived at his destination. As they were every time he went off on mental tangents about Olivia or the baby that week. Which was pretty much anytime he wasn't completely focused on something else. Every night as he went to bed, he ticked off another day of no bad news. If Beth lost the baby, he'd get a call. His newly signed paperwork assured him of that.

Olivia had told him his role was completely up to him.

And that she needed to know what that role was going to be. At least there'd be no money worries.

That felt good. So he opened an investment account specifically for nonessential savings for the child. He'd already done so for college. And another one for health expenses.

As the week progressed he found himself taking a private poll of every man he had a conversation with—a cabdriver, a doorman, his business associates, a bartender, friends... He couldn't seem to stop himself from asking if they had kids. And then encouraging them to discuss the experience. He was good at drawing people out. Getting them to reveal things without realizing that he was doing more than serving up small talk. He'd never, ever used the talent to find out about fatherhood. Or lack thereof. And mostly all he got was a fistful of envy for the guys who were comfortable in their paternal shoes, and the other fist full of sympathy for the guys who weren't—whether they had kids and weren't involved, or didn't have children. The one group he didn't feel much for, other than a lack of respect, were the guys who had families and didn't seem all that interested in them.

By the time Sunday noon rolled around and he was sitting in his parked vehicle, waiting for Olivia at the beach parking lot, he'd run out of time.

She wanted to know who he was going to be in their future.

He had absolutely no idea what he wanted, what he felt. How could he have no idea?

He always had ideas. Always knew what to do. Or where to get the information to figure it out.

He'd been gathering information all week and he didn't know what to do. Who he could be. Should be. Would be good at being. Didn't have any idea how he ensured that Olivia and the baby were happy.

He certainly hadn't been able to do a damned thing to ease Lily's suffering. Or Olivia's. His presence hadn't been able to bring happiness to either one of them. His power, his money...

He'd worked so hard to achieve them, to have security and enough money to raise his kids with wonderful memories and happy times. And when the time had come, neither power nor money had mattered a whit.

A red SUV pulled up next to him and a man in jeans and a long-sleeved T-shirt got out. He looked to be late twenties or so with sandy hair. He opened the door directly behind his and bent to a car seat, pulling out a boy big enough to start hopping around as soon as he was on the ground. Pretty soon a woman in leggings and a long sweatshirt, with her blond hair in a ponytail, joined him with a baby on her hip. The little boy said something. Martin couldn't make out the words, but he heard the excitement in the child's voice as his father pulled a cooler out of the back of the vehicle and handed a blanket to the woman.

A family on a Sunday picnic. He should envy them. And didn't. They were them, living their lives. He was living his. They were starting out, with a lifetime ahead of them for building who they'd become. He'd already become.

With the cooler in one hand, the dad reached down a hand and the little boy slid his small fingers inside it. Martin looked away, having trouble swallowing.

And his passenger door swung open.

"Sorry I'm late. I had a call from the hospital about a patient I've been following closely..." Olivia said, setting her purse on the floor at her feet as she slid inside. In skinny dress pants and a tailored off-white button-up cotton top, with her hair down, she turned his world on end. Again.

Every single time he saw her.

And, as usual, he pretended she didn't.

How did a guy keep doing that for the rest of his life?

"Everything okay?" he asked, knowing she couldn't give him specifics about any patient.

He used to resent that. Hated that her work with at-risk babies affected her so deeply and she couldn't share any of it with him.

Eventually he'd realized that the law only accounted for a small portion of the things Olivia didn't share with him anymore. Or hadn't shared, since they'd gotten divorced.

"As good as can be expected," she told him in answer to his question, and he examined her, trying to read between the lines. Was she losing a baby at work?

"You look like you're going to meet the president," she said, glancing up and down his frame, giving him the beginning of a hard-on.

"I could have come from church," he said to defend the navy dress pants, white shirt and navy-and-white tie he'd chosen for the occasion.

"Did you?"

"No."

She grinned. He wanted to kiss her.

And put the SUV in gear.

Olivia had arranged to meet Beth and Brian at their house, hoping to meet the rest of the family, but Beth's aunt and sister had taken the kids to the park and out for ice cream. The fresh air was good for her aunt, Beth mentioned as she walked Martin and Olivia through the modest home and out to a patio that opened out to a small yard with freshly cut grass completely closed in by a block wall that attached to both sides of the house.

As she and Martin sat on a wicker love seat, Brian came out carrying a tray with glasses and individual-size juice bottles of various flavors. The couple, both in jeans, T-shirts and flip-flops, sat on the love seat opposite them, with the tray on the little table between the two couches.

Olivia made the introductions, leaving out the part

about Martin being a techie guru millionaire entre-
preneur. Everyone was smiling. Polite. On best be-
havior. And yet she wanted to run.

Which made no sense. She truly liked Beth and
Brian and would have even if they hadn't been in the
process of bringing her baby to life. What she didn't
like was knowing that they had to be sizing up Martin. Watching her. Wondering about the relationship
between them.

Wondering how the baby was going to fit into it.

Beth, in particular. While the embryo she was carrying wasn't hers, the pregnancy was. Her body—
her hormones, her emotions and maternal instincts,
her protective instincts—would be in full gear. She
was going to love Olivia's child. There was just no
getting around that one.

Martin made small talk. Asked about Brian's job
as an EMT. About Beth's teaching. He asked about
their own children. Complimented them on their
house when Olivia knew the place was barely as
fancy as his garage. And probably about the same
size, too.

He did what he was good at and she was thankful to have him there.

Until he suddenly blurted, "I'd like to be present
for the first ultrasound, and for the birth, as well. Is
that going to present a problem?" He included both
Brian and Beth in the question.

They'd had fifteen minutes in the car on the way

over and he hadn't thought to mention that little tidbit to her?

Granted, she'd told him he could be as involved as he chose, told him he was going to have to decide his level of involvement all on his own, but…

She'd also asked him to inform her when he knew…

And did it mean that he planned to be present after the baby's birth? Was he going to be more than a provider to her child? Was he thinking he might actually want to be involved in their lives?

She stared at him, her heart pumping hard, feeling as though she was back on the precipice she'd stood on so often with him in the past. Was it okay to want him around?

Or was the wanting only going to hurt them both?

If they were careful to keep their involvement only about the baby, could they make it work?

Brian and Beth had been looking at each other, as though speaking in silent language, and when Brian nodded, Beth looked at Martin. "That's fine," she said. "The father should definitely have a right to be present to hear his child's heartbeat for the first time. And for the birth."

"Thank you." Martin smiled. "I'll be circumspect, you have my word on that. I'll respect your privacy. I'd just like to be in the room."

The younger couple nodded in unison.

"You're not showing yet," Martin said next, and

Olivia stared at him. Had the man lost his mind? And his tact?

"Nope. It's only been a few weeks. I'll be a month along on Friday." Five days away.

"Are you feeling any morning sickness?"

Olivia had with Lily from the second week. They'd almost had to hospitalize her because she couldn't keep anything down. And then she'd suddenly had the appetite of a seven-foot athlete.

"Nope." Beth shook her head.

Sliding his hand into hers, Brian said, "She didn't get sick at all with our other two kids, so we're hoping it's that easy for her this time."

And so it went. The conversation was intimate and chatty at the same time. Strangers discussing personal details of pregnancy. As Olivia sat there, mostly listening, but speaking up occasionally, too, she had to do a mental shake or two to believe this was even happening.

Her first meeting with Beth and Brian had taken place in a medical facility and she hadn't even thought she was seriously considering surrogacy at that moment. Hadn't been ready to admit to herself that she was going to do whatever it took to bring her baby to life.

She'd still been reeling from what she'd done. Trying to come to terms with why.

And there she was, less than four weeks later, with her whole world changed because of one night of incredible sex.

* * *

Martin liked the couple Olivia had chosen to have her baby. Brian, with his short blond hair and clean-shaven face, reminded him of himself when he was younger. Responsible. Dedicated to his wife and family.

"As an EMT, Brian will know what to do in an event of an emergency with the baby," he told Olivia as they drove back to her car, focusing on the good stuff in an effort to ward off the conversation he knew had to be coming. He'd insinuated himself into more than they'd talked about back there. Needed a second to figure out why before answering to her on it. "I thought we'd be there around fifteen minutes, not an hour."

Nor had he pictured them leaving with an invitation to come back in ten days to share Thanksgiving dinner with the family, to meet Beth's aunt and sister. Olivia hadn't declined right away, saying they'd have to check and get back with them, but he knew she'd get them out of it.

"Beth is a nurturer," Olivia said in response to his EMT comment. He'd thought he was reassuring her about the safety of the baby, to put her worries at ease in any small manner he could. She seemed to have missed the plus in their favor with that one.

Turning off the Applegates' street, he tried to find a way to broach the fact that he'd failed to come up with the perimeters of his boundaries where the baby was concerned. He didn't want her to think it wasn't a priority.

Or to know that he was completely lost for the first time in his life.

"It would have been nice to have a heads-up about the ultrasound and…stuff," she said while his brain scrambled for appropriate verbiage to convey that which he didn't have to convey. Or want to convey.

"What do you mean?" he asked, hedging his bets that he was about to be in the thick of it, with no way out.

Looking at him, and not smilingly, he could tell even from peripheral vision, she said, "You couldn't let me know that you wanted to be there for the ultrasound and birth before you sprung it on them? When I hired them, I told them that you weren't going to be involved at all."

"But…they knew that had changed." His visit had made that more than apparent.

"You told me you'd let me know."

He nodded. Pulled off into a vacant parking lot of some kind of professional building. Palm trees dotted squared-off portions of the lot, an attempt to beautify, he figured. Was pretty sure they were completely lost on his ex-wife.

"Look," he said, still belted in, facing forward. "I know I said I'd let you know—" he looked over at her, sitting there so straight and serious and beautiful "—and I will. I just… I don't know yet, Liv. I'm sorry. I just…"

Her expression didn't soften with his honesty. "You knew you wanted to be in the ultrasound."

"No, I didn't!" Forget the ultrasound already. His problem wasn't a medical exam. It was…the whole picture. "I just… While we were sitting there, and I'm thinking about what she's doing for us, remembering our pregnancy and what we are asking of the two of them…it occurred to me that there'd be an ultrasound and that I should be there."

Because if something went wrong, he couldn't let Olivia face it alone. If there was no heartbeat. If something went wrong at the birth. If the baby didn't breathe. Or was…in trouble as Lily had been.

She frowned. "You hadn't thought of that ahead of time? You just made the choice when you asked them the question?"

"That's right."

She examined him, and then the lines in her face softened. Her gaze softened.

"Would you rather I not be there?" he asked. He'd have a hard time staying away, because of Olivia, and for the baby, too, but if that was what she wanted, he'd do so.

"Of course not! If you want to be there, I definitely think you should be."

"But do *you* want me there?"

"As long as you want to be there, yes."

How had they gotten to a point of having to clarify every little thing before they could commit to an honest feeling? How had he not noticed?

He didn't like it.

Didn't want that kind of relationship between them. Didn't like the possibility that it was his own indecision causing a big part of it.

"I want to be there," he said. No clarifying.

And he felt good for a second when she smiled.

Chapter Thirteen

Didn't seem to matter that she was a successful trauma specialist. When she was around Martin she felt…less in charge. Of her life. Of her emotions. Because those led her places her brain knew it was better not to go and then she had to deal with the consequences.

When he was around, she wanted to throw caution to the wind. As a young woman she'd ignored Sylvia's warnings, and those of her friends, too, taking up with a man so much older than her. In the end, they'd all been proven right.

She'd given in to emotion that fateful Friday night just over a month ago, and there she was, riding in her ex-husband's car, less than three weeks after they'd agreed never to see each other again, talking about ultrasounds.

"I'm assuming you're going to get us out of Thanksgiving," Martin said as he turned onto the major thoroughfare that would take them to the beach parking lot.

She'd brought clothes to go for a run—something she hadn't done in far too long. Something she'd done in high school and college and given up because Martin wasn't into it.

"I'll get you out of it," she said, immediately tamping down on the "us" in his sentence. "I'm sure you've got stuff happening, but I think I'm going to go." She was certain of it actually. Made up her mind, right then and there.

"What about Sylvia?"

"I'll invite her along." Her heart lifted a bit as she seriously thought about the upcoming holiday. The past few years she and Sylvia had had a quiet dinner at home and then gone for a drive along the coastal highway before doing some late-night Black Friday shopping at a favorite mall near Mission Viejo. Not all that far from the Applegates'.

"Don't you think you should check with them first?" He wasn't smiling now. "They don't know her."

"Of course I'll call Beth, but I'm sure she'll be fine with it." He never had been all that fond of her mother. Partially because Sylvia hadn't approved of him being with her daughter—for good reason, as it turned out—and partially, Olivia had always thought, because Sylvia being so close to his age made him feel too old for her. "And they already know her. She was with me the day I met them."

He frowned then. Glanced her way. "I should have been there."

"You were in Italy," she reminded him. And hadn't bothered to call when she'd texted asking him to do so. Not that they needed to go over all that again. They were on different wavelengths, in different places. It's just the way it was. "And it's fine this way, too," she continued, trying to help him find his way. Needing to help him where she could.

The thought of him even needing her help at all was so new she still wasn't sure if it was something she was conjuring in her own brain to justify needing him. She added, "Sylvia's going to be a major part of the baby's life. She's the only grandparent this baby's going to have. So it's right that she spends time with Beth, too. The baby needs to know her voice."

He'd pulled into the parking lot. Put the SUV in Park and turned to face her. "What?" he asked.

"That's one of the reasons I'm spending time with Beth, and in her home," she said, giving him information only as he asked for it. Because she wasn't going to pressure him or drag him back in. She really could do this without him. She had not one doubt about that.

Her doubts came from how much she wanted him involved. She wanted her baby to know him because she knew he'd make an incredible father. Seeing his loyalty and dedication to the Fishnet kids showed her that. But she wanted it for him, too. And for herself.

"There's a lot of evidence that babies take in environmental sounds, and sometimes emotions, from outside the womb as they're growing. It's why they know their mother's voice and the others' in their families.

It helps them adjust to life in the outside world after they're born. Since this baby isn't going to be going home to Beth and Brian, I want the baby to know my voice, the voices of those in my family, to ease the transition…"

To feel safe with her.

And, if she let herself think about it, to sense that she was his or her mother. At least a little bit. To recognize her voice. To look in her direction when he or she heard her voice, as Lily had done.

"You never mentioned this with the first pregnancy."

"I didn't know as much then. And we were there, together every morning and night—the baby knew our voices. This is different because I'm not there."

She wasn't the one nurturing her child. Didn't have a changing body. Wasn't going to feel her baby move. A wave of deep sadness swept through her and she let it pass. Her embryo needed her positive energy and thoughts. Needed everything she had to give to see it born safe and healthy. This wasn't about her.

And if she got a miracle—and they'd made it through two big hurdles on their way to one—then she was going to be a mother again. To her own biological child. Fertilized in her body.

"I have a Thanksgiving dinner at Fishnet," Martin was saying. "Our LA facility has grown and I offered to man a spot on the serving line, to give the kids a true family feel."

Because he was the "father" of them all. She got what Martin had done. He'd taken the loss of his daughter, the loss of his world, and made something wonderful out of his life from the ashes. He'd created a family larger than any he'd ever have created with a wife. And yet, he'd done it while mostly on the outside of the sphere. He oversaw. He didn't generally interact personally with the kids who were the nucleus of that family.

"Then absolutely you should be there," she told him, glad that he'd actually volunteered to be a part of the celebration. And was kind of turned on, thinking of him standing behind a long table with an apron covering his expensive clothes and a spoon in his hand. Just the vision of it. Some women went for naked bodies. She apparently liked men fully clothed with an apron on and spoon in hand.

"I need to be at the Applegates'," he said, shaking his head. "The child should know my voice, too."

Not if he wasn't going to be a father to it. Children didn't need to know the people bankrolling their existence. She didn't respond to his comment.

"I'm listed on the paperwork," he continued as she just sat there. It occurred to her then that she should have used the silence to open the door and get out. She'd encouraged more from him by just sitting there.

"If anything happened to you, I'd have rights... I'd be the sole support."

She didn't get out of the car. And didn't speak. Just waited for him to work it out however he had to.

"I should be there for the holiday," he said. "The mood will be festive. It'll be a family gathering with loving feelings. My voice should be accounted for."

She didn't disagree. Just wasn't sure what they were getting into. Where it was all going to lead.

If Martin chose to be an involved father, she didn't worry for a second about him reneging on that. It wasn't his way at all. If he made the choice, he'd be there for their child. But did she want him to make that choice?

She honestly didn't know what she wanted where he was concerned.

Because, other than her work, she hadn't dared to want anything for a long time. The thought struck her cold.

"I'll call Marsha and Sam Bruins, live-in house parents for the sixteen- and seventeen-year-old area, and let them know I can't make it."

"You need to make it," she said then. "What time is dinner there?"

"Five. We made it later because some of the kids are in food service and have to work."

"Beth and Brian are having dinner at two," she said. And then, without thought, suggested, "We could do their house and then I could go with you to Fishnet."

Why in the hell she'd needed to do that, she had

no idea. Except that he was clearly struggling, alone, clearly trying, and if she could offer support…

"What about Sylvia?"

"If you wouldn't mind, I'd invite her to help at Fishnet, as well. I know she'd enjoy doing so."

While her mother still believed Olivia's marriage to Martin had been a mistake, she had come to understand how much Olivia had loved him. And now that, through Olivia, she knew him better, she most definitely admired all that he'd done with his life.

What she thought of him since Beth had been implanted with their embryo, Olivia had no idea. Her mother had been busier than normal the past month and, when they'd met for dinner, had only talked about Olivia. About the baby. About being a grandmother and being involved every step of the way. About being a good mother to her daughter who was going to be a mother…

"Okay."

Olivia's gaze shot to Martin. He'd always hated being around her mother. Or rather, had always chosen not to be around her any chance he got. "Okay?" she asked, trying to read the expression in his eyes.

His gaze warm, not quite smiling, but seemingly at ease, he nodded. "Okay."

And she felt guilty. "You should know, the baby's ears won't be fully formed yet. They don't actually hear sound until around the eighteenth week of pregnancy. As far as anyone can tell or prove. I just want to be there from the beginning. And even though it most likely can't hear anything yet, the fetus can feel Beth's emotions, or her emotions can have an effect on it, and I'd like her to feel like I'm there, being a good mom. A part of things…"

He nodded. "Fine. Thanks for the clarification. I'd still like to be there."

Well, then, her world was definitely changing. She wasn't opposing the changes, but didn't trust them, either. Didn't trust them to be what she thought. Or to not go wrong. Which meant she had to hold on tight to her heart.

And pray that she didn't get thrown from the galloping horse she seemed to be riding.

Sylvia couldn't make it to Thanksgiving. While Martin wasn't surprised, Olivia seemed a bit bothered by her mother's refusal.

"She said she has a friend whose spouse died not that long ago with whom she wanted to spend the day," Olivia had told Martin. He hadn't heard from her since dropping her off at her car more than a week before, other than the text he'd requested once she got back to Marie Cove safely that afternoon.

And while he'd thought of her every day and wanted to pick up his phone and at least text, he didn't do so. She wasn't actually pregnant, carrying the baby, so no excuse to check up. Right? And until he knew he was going to be in her life—if he was going to be in her life or just the baby's, or just be a financier unless they needed him—until he knew something…he didn't want to build anything.

More than anything, he wasn't going to let her down.

He'd choose death over causing her to suffer. Melodramatic, maybe, but most days that was how he felt.

Because they were traveling to multiple places, and ending up at Fishnet, they'd agreed to meet at Martin's home, where she could leave her car, and they could drive together to the Applegates'. She'd suggested he find himself a pair of jeans for the occasion, paired with a casually nice sweater, and though he might not have chosen the outfit himself, he felt okay in it as he answered the door to her just after noon on Thanksgiving Thursday.

In brown leggings and a cotton blouse with a pattern of fall-colored shapes that fell to just above midthigh, and brown flats, she stepped inside his door as though she belonged there. So he could be forgiven for the instant sense that she did belong that was flooding over him. He couldn't allow that to continue, though, and went to collect his keys and phone.

She was in the kitchen when he returned, standing with her hand suspended down toward the handle of the cupboard under the sink. With her hair thick and silky-looking as it flowed over her, and the large, dark eyes and tan complexion, she looked like an angel to him, slowing him down for a second.

"I had a mint," she said, holding up the wrapper. "I went to throw it away, but the door wouldn't open."

She was staring at him, the wrapper still suspended, almost as though she'd forgotten it.

"I had the place babyproofed last week," he told her, grabbing the wrapper and getting it in the trash without looking her way again. "A service came in. I saved their card for you, in case you wanted to use them."

Reaching into his back pocket, he grabbed his wallet, and then the card.

Openmouthed, she was still standing there, watching his every move. He felt her stare, felt her questions.

In hindsight, he probably could have waited until after the first trimester passed to have the work done.

"You aren't even sure how involved you want to be and you've had the condo babyproofed?"

"In case of emergency," he enunciated clearly. "If for any reason you need help or, say, just have appendicitis or something…"

"My mom will babysit," she told him. "And Christine would, too."

Right. She had it all covered. He was proud of her. Relieved, even. And yet he couldn't just stand back and let her be. No, he had to insert himself… "You know me," he joked. "Always prepared."

She could possibly buy it. He'd always gone over-board to anticipate any need she might have and make certain that he'd done all he could do to ful-fill it. To the point of suffocating her, he supposed.

"You don't have to justify yourself to me, Martin," she finally said, taking the card and putting it in the small, black zippered purse she always carried, then she moved toward the door. "If you want the baby to come here, all you have to do is say so."

"I'm not saying that."

"I know."

Did she? He tried to meet her gaze, but she was the one avoiding him that time.

Olivia was excited to see the Applegates again. To be close to her fetus. To know that when she spoke the sound might reach the baby in some fashion, a vibration even. And the surrogate could soak up Olivia's energy, too.

As a doctor and scientist, she knew, more than most, how miracles happened, and they weren't through anything she or her colleagues had learned or done.

The turkey was out of the oven and dinner was ready to be served by the time they got there, home-made pies in hand. After the rest of the introductions—Beth's aunt and sister to Olivia and Martin, and the kids, three and seven, who mostly just wanted to be able to play their video games in the family room—the conversation was general. No talk of the baby Beth was carrying. Just people getting to know each other better and feeling thankful—each in their own personal way.

The kids both chatted through dinner, asking questions, making note of what they did and didn't like. Olivia liked that they were comfortable speaking up at the table. She'd always thought a family dinner table should be free for all—a place where, hopefully, the children would bring to the adults anything going on in their lives.

Her grandmother had always insisted they have dinner together, even when it had to wait until Olivia was off work from the job at the fast-food restaurant she'd taken in high school, and they didn't actually eat until nine or later. And Olivia had always replayed her day for her grandmother at that same table.

She'd been seated next to Martin at dinner, across from Beth's aunt and sister, but when dishes were done and it was time for dessert in front of the TV, she noticed Beth's aunt, who'd been watching the football game, on one side of Martin, and Brian on the other. The kids were on the floor with bowls of vanilla ice cream, so Olivia joined them. She was good with kids. Comfortable.

And she had a view of Martin and "Aunt Wendy" as they chatted about players and stats. And enjoyed Olivia's pie.

"I've always been a 49ers fan," Wendy was saying. "Ever since the Joe Montana days."

Olivia had no idea who Joe Montana was.

"And the Chicago Bears were next," Wendy continued, while a commercial played out on the set and Beth and her sister were still occupied in the kitchen. The kids were discussing who had the biggest glob on their spoon. "I'd watched Jim Harbaugh play for Michigan and was thrilled when he was drafted by Chicago."

Jim Harbaugh was the football coach at Michigan, she knew. Because one of the little ones she'd cared for, a boy who'd gone home just the week before, had been born a Michigan fan. His parents had put up blue and maize all around his bassinet, and every Saturday his father would have the game on, giving the baby a play-by-play of what was going on. It was the man's way of coping. She'd recognized that, and so had taken an interest.

He'd failed to mention that the Michigan coach had once been a famous professional player. Or even that he'd quarterbacked for the college team he now coached.

But Martin and Wendy both knew. They'd both watched him play, in college and in Chicago. Sometime before she'd been born. He'd gone on to play for other professional teams, too, when she'd been alive, but still a little girl. Olivia heard it all.

When Wendy's hand landed on Martin's arm as she was exclaiming over something some announcer had said ages before, Olivia got up and left the room.

Martin was a charmer. In the best sense of the word. He was genuinely a nice guy. She'd never met anyone who didn't like him. Or anyone he couldn't engage in conversation.

But he was also a man. And Wendy was most clearly a woman who'd become charmed.

It didn't matter. Wendy wasn't the only woman who found Martin attractive. She knew that he was invited to functions where the hosts evened the numbers with a female partner for him on occasion. Knew he still had sex.

That didn't mean she wanted to witness the effects of his charisma.

Or be reminded of the fact that there were other women in his life.

She wasn't jealous, she promised herself. She wasn't.

Martin wasn't hers. They weren't happy together. She wanted him to be happy.

Honestly.

And honestly, she was burning with jealousy, too.

Over something she couldn't have and wouldn't accept if it were offered to her.

Maybe she wasn't as ready for a changing world as she'd hoped.

Chapter Fourteen

"Wendy sure looked good." Martin was making small talk as he pulled out of the parking lot of the Fishnet three-floor dormitory-style boardinghouse later that evening. "You'd never know she's in dire need of a liver."

Something was up with Olivia. She'd been pleasant but wearing what he could only figure was her bedside manner since dessert at the Applegates' that afternoon. And at Fishnet, she'd been polite, kind, did all that was asked of her with a smile as she stood at the end of the row of food pans and served dressing to the teenagers coming through their line. She'd had dinner with a table of eight girls and by the looks of things they'd been enthralled with her. But there'd been no laughing. She'd sat up straight the whole time and insisted on helping with dishes rather than relaxing in the huge, living-room-style lounge with the kids to watch *Miracle on 34th Street*.

She hadn't met his gaze one time since they'd been passing mashed potatoes, sitting next to each other at Beth and Brian's table.

Until he could figure out what was bothering her, he'd keep her talking.

Distract her, if nothing else.

Because there were some things you couldn't fix. Like a baby too sick to live. A relationship that had broken when they'd needed it most. Like the fact that his ex-wife had spent the afternoon with the woman who was pregnant with her baby. Because she couldn't carry her baby herself. It had to be hard.

While he'd heard that some women didn't particularly enjoy pregnancy, were uncomfortable and just wanted it done with, Olivia had been a natural at it. She'd been so happy, touching her stomach all the time, marveling at every new moment. The first time she couldn't fasten her jeans. The first time she could feel the baby move. And later, when they'd actually been able to see a bump move across her belly as the foot or fist moved…

His comment regarding Beth's aunt's looks hadn't elicited a response.

"I expected her to be frail," he added. He'd been expecting her to be nearly bedridden. Or in a wheelchair.

"She has a cirrhosis that is terminal to liver function," she responded. "It hasn't yet progressed to the point of making her look jaundiced, but the longer they wait to do the transplant, the more risk there will be to her overall health. If they can get it done while she's still relatively healthy and able to manage symptoms with medicine, the better chance there is that her body will accept the new liver."

More than he needed to know. As were the next paragraphs of medical terminology that came at him regarding overall liver function, disease and treatment. He was reminded just how far she'd climbed in the world since their divorce, though. Impressed as hell by what she'd become. "The liver is one of the few organs that regenerates itself," she said. "So the donor can lose part of a healthy liver and not miss it."

She was talking to him. Not staring silently out the side window as she'd done most of the way from the Applegates' to Fishnet.

"So, in your opinion, I know you can't give me specifics about a particular patient, but in your opinion, based on Wendy's age, and assuming she's overall healthy, this procedure could possibly allow her to live a normal life span?"

The woman had clearly been integral to the Applegate family. He'd like to think long life was an option. He'd like to think that Beth and her sister's sacrifices wouldn't be in vain.

"Yes."

Her response was followed by an immediate turn of her head toward the side window.

What the hell?

"What's bothering you?"

"Nothing."

"Come on, Liv. Tell me it's none of my business, but don't lie to me. Surely we haven't come to that?"

Her silence was better than a lie, he supposed.

And let it hang there between them the rest of the way to his place. She didn't owe him her thoughts. She didn't owe him anything.

But as the few miles passed far too quickly and he pulled into the garage of his condo and knew that her car was going to be pulling out momentarily, he couldn't just let the silence continue to separate them.

If any more came between them, they might not find a way to make anything work. Which would maybe be the right thing if it was just the two of them.

He put the SUV in Park, but left it running. "There's a baby on the way," he said, wishing he could read her mind even half as well as he used to think he could. "We're going to be facing some intense situations—individually and together—and while I admit I'm not coming up with answers here, I do know that we have to be honest with each other or this whole thing could explode in a way neither of us want. In a way that couldn't possibly be good for a child."

She glanced at him then, some life back in her gaze, but he couldn't decipher any message she might be throwing at him. She didn't look angry. But it wasn't good.

In their olden days, he'd have guessed, anyway.

And kept guessing until he found something he could fix.

He'd since realized that hadn't been fair to her. She wasn't his to fix. Either it would come from her, or it wouldn't. The choice was entirely hers.

And, as it had turned out back then, anyway, even when he'd known what had needed fixing— her uterus, their daughter's body—he hadn't been able to do a damned thing about either one of them. No amount of money or hard work in the world could help.

Possibilities are endless if you give it your all and work hard enough, his parents had always said. Refusing to accept any excuses in their home. Pushing him to be the best version of himself. And when it had counted most, when his family had needed help, he'd had nothing.

"Sometimes silence is better than honesty." Her voice was like a husky-sounding siren filling the car. His ears.

The doctor was no longer with them.

"What's going on?" The question was pulled from him by the sad look in her eyes that was directed straight at him.

Like he had something to do with what was bothering her. Or was indirectly involved at least. Was she making plans for his role in the child's life since he'd failed to do so in a timely enough fashion?

Was she going to keep him from the baby because he couldn't commit to who or what he was going to be?

"I'm jealous of Wendy."

His mind stopped. Her words frozen in place there.

"Jealous, how?" he asked eventually, realizing it was up to him to draw her out, or remain sitting there, with them staring at each other, going nowhere.

"Is there more than one way to be jealous?"

She wasn't smiling. Was completely serious.

He'd asked for the truth.

"Why would you be jealous of her?" he asked. "Because she's Beth's aunt and will be around all the time so the baby can hear her voice as its ears develop?"

"Because you and she…"

He shook his head and she broke off.

He should have let her finish. Refused to let himself speak.

"She can sit there with you and flirt and she gets to be the recipient of your charm and—"

"Are you saying that's something you want for yourself?" His penis started to grow hard as his heartbeat revved up.

When she shook her head, his system took a nosedive. And then she shrugged. "We've been there, done that. It didn't work for us. Doesn't work for us."

He nodded. Unable to deny the truth of that. The

pain their union had caused them…and not for lack of trying to make it work from both sides…

"And it wasn't just that," she said, her eyes glistening now. "You were talking about things that you'd shared, even though you'd never met each other before. You could relate on a personal level to how she felt about Michigan's coach. You bonded over that shared reality. And it was all a blank page to me. I had no idea Harbaugh ever played for Michigan."

"I had no idea you knew Michigan's coach's name." She'd had zero interest in football. And he was homing in on what did not matter. He got it. Held there, anyway.

She told him about a recent patient whose father had been a fan. He heard her describe things the dad brought into the boy's area of the NICU to give the baby a more personal, nursery-like feel. And tried to find a way to make the decade that he'd been alive before her not matter.

"You grew up on cassettes," she said. "I grew up on CDs."

Different frames of reference. He got that. A lot of couples made it work. Or some did. He sure as hell hadn't been the first man to marry a younger woman. There were couples in LA with decades' differences in their ages. And not all of them with the man being the older of the two.

He could argue it all. Had argued it all internally many, many times.

None of his valid points had fixed the problems between him and Olivia. No matter what other couples did or did not do for each other, or wanted out of a marriage, or decided to settle for, he and Olivia both knew what they wanted and needed, and those didn't mesh.

He knew this. Had told himself a million times over and over and over again.

They were right where they'd ended up, again. Every time. No matter what road they traveled. They kept coming back. They couldn't find their way out of the circular path, but hadn't been able to let it go, either.

Which was why he'd broken things off with her.

"You asked for the truth." Her brows raised, as though she was pleading for mercy. Or apologizing.

He nodded.

"So...there you have it. I'm jealous of you with other women. Most particularly women your own age or older. Women who lived when you did before I was born. Women who can share your perspective."

Wait...what? She was jealous of him with all other women? Even Wendy, because they could converse easily without the tension of a failed relationship between them?

She didn't want him with other women?

The idea gave him an immediate sense of great satisfaction. Of course, he'd always been bothered by the idea of her with other men, but had figured that had just been him.

"I'm not sure what good this honesty serves," she continued. "So now can we agree that sometimes us staying silent will serve the baby better?"

"You're jealous, as in, you don't want me but you don't want anyone else to have me, either? As in, if you can't have it no one else should?"

It wasn't an emotion to be proud of, but it was real. People felt envy. What mattered was what they did with that.

Olivia was dealing with it.

She shook her head slightly. Stared at him in the shadows left after the overhead garage light went off, her features lit only by the security light.

"I'm jealous because I *do* want you, and can't have you," she said. "I've been struggling with it all night. How do I see you like this, have you in my life, and not want you?"

All systems were on full alert without warning, driving all other thoughts out of his brain except joining their bodies and hearing her cry out with the pleasure he knew he could bring her.

"When I see you out with other people, I see how kind you are, how you always make other people comfortable, draw them out, make them feel good about themselves and yet be genuine at the same time, and then I see a particular look in your eye, or the way your hair curls—it's like it's always been for me with you. I want you so badly…"

Oh God, he wanted her, too. Even worse.

"And then I remember what it was like at home, when we were faced with everyday life…when it was more than just who we were, or how attracted we were, when all the little things started to matter."

"I want you, too, Liv. What you just said, about how you feel when we're out together, seeing you with others—it lights a fire in me that burns me up."

He couldn't tell if she was pleased with his admission or not. She licked her lips. He needed to kiss them. She didn't move forward, but didn't tear her gaze away, either.

"So…are we saying that you were right to break us off a few weeks ago? That we can't see each other anymore? In spite of the baby?"

He wasn't saying anything like that.

At least, not intentionally.

"Because what we do to each other, that can't be a healthy environment for a child. To have its parents attracted to one another, but unable to share a life."

He couldn't see a way for that to be healthy for any of them.

"But…depending on your level of involvement… maybe it would be better for the baby if you and I could make some kind of plan so that you can still have access. I mean, having you as some kind of presence in the baby's life… Even if that just means

I keep you apprised of the child's well-being in any event that you'd need to be more of a figure in his or her life. Wouldn't that be better for that child than for your relationship to just be nonexistent?"

Her tone sounded as though the doctor had returned. But the glint in her eyes as she held his gaze steadily was anything but medically induced.

"What are you saying?"

She sighed. "I really don't know," she told him. "I don't want to pressure you to be anything, or do anything, but when I think about us just arbitrarily deciding we can't be together, and cutting you out of any possibility with our baby…it just…"

Her lips trembled, her eyes starting to squint like she might start to cry.

"I don't see a way out for us, Liv," he told her, but had to continue. "I've been doing a lot of thinking, and one thing that's become clear is that our original plan, or mine at least, to get on with our lives, for me to find a partner, all of that…well, it's not going to play out as I'd intended. Clearly. The child exists. It's half mine. I can't walk away from that. And that changes the plan."

He felt like he was rambling. Was playing things out as they came to him. But finally, something concrete was coming.

He reached out a hand. Touched her face lightly, and she turned her lips into his palm. Not kissing him, just…touching. A hello? A goodbye?

He couldn't tell her goodbye. Not tonight.

"We've limped along for the past nine years," he said softly, holding her cheek, needing to hold so much more of her. "Maybe we limp for the next eighteen or so…"

Her gaze was tender, vulnerable, as she looked at him. "Is it wise?"

"I don't know."

"We should probably think about it…"

He nodded.

"Can I stay tonight, Martin? It might not be wise, or best, or healthy. But one more time… I need your arms around me so badly. Everything's coming so fast, and there you were, sitting there talking to Wendy and… I need to feel you inside me."

Still holding her face, he lowered his lips to hers. Intending to kiss her gently, and somehow ending up gathering her as close as the console would allow and consuming her mouth.

Desperate to be consumed by her.

Chapter Fifteen

Olivia couldn't resist him. She could save babies' lives. She could raise a child on her own. But that Thanksgiving night, she couldn't pull out of her ex-husband's arms.

He gave her a chance to go. More than one chance.

The first as he'd left the car and stood aside while she climbed down not far from the driver's door of her shiny white BMW. She had her purse. Her keys. The garage door was still open.

And she'd walked straight up to him, pushing her body against his, and planted her lips on his, sticking her tongue into his mouth.

In the elevator, she'd crossed the foot of distance he'd left between them and pressed her pelvis up against his burgeoning fly. Rubbing herself on him in a way she knew drove him to distraction.

And once they were inside his condo, she didn't wait until they got to his bedroom before she started unbuttoning his shirt. And hers.

It didn't matter that they couldn't live together, that daily life was a problem for them. That they needed different things. At the moment they needed exactly the same thing.

And she needed it worse than she needed to re-member any of the rest of it. She wasn't signing on for a lifetime or making decisions for anything but the moment.

"Are you sure?" he asked as they landed on the sectional in front of his entertainment center. "The last time…"

She kissed his words silent. And then, still half-dressed, and sitting right on top of the fly of his pants, she stopped. He was so gorgeous, his eyes that saw so much but hid so much of what he knew. The nose that gave him authority somehow. The lips that smiled and approved and kissed like a hungry lion. The slight bit of silver at his temples giving him a distinction that only turned her on more…

"I don't want the last time to be the last time," she said, finding it hard to keep pushing truths down in-side her. And knowing that as badly as she needed to be one with him, to find a release for the passion he'd always raised in her, she couldn't be reckless again. "I'm not saying anything about the future," she told him. "I'm in such a deep sense of 'wait and see' that I couldn't guarantee that anything I'd say tonight would still ring true to me next week. Not where all of this is concerned."

"What are you saying?" he asked softly, giving her his full attention.

He was still hard beneath her backside. She could feel him, even through their pants. But he was no longer pressing up against her. Her shirt hung open. His was off, on the floor somewhere between them and the door. The front clasp of her lacy bra was undone, the sides hanging half over her breasts.

"I don't want the last time to be our last time," she said again, certain of what she was feeling, but not sure why. "I don't want conception to define the end of…it."

"I ended it before I knew about any possible conception."

"I know," she said, and nodded, her long hair falling over her breasts, tickling them as she moved her head. "I was out of sorts, emotionally tied up, reckless. I was looking for escape…"

"You were using me."

Maybe. It hadn't felt that way at the time.

"Is that what we've done over the years? Used each other?" She wasn't judging either one of them.

"No."

She hadn't thought so, either.

"We do something for each other, Martin. Right or wrong, good or bad. Maybe we can't do it anymore. Maybe we'll never be able to stop. All I know is that I want you so badly I ache. And that I can't stand the thought of the baby's conception and the last time we're ever going to be together being the same night. It doesn't feel good."

It tainted the baby somehow.

"I'm not saying there's any logic to it. But I can tell you the thought has been bothering me for a few weeks. I need it all separate in my mind. I need to be able to tell our child that her conception, or his, wasn't the last time we were together. Or that it was just a one-time thing." The words started to come more clearly as she saw the raw interest in his gaze. He was really listening.

"Not that I plan to report, but I'd want to know. I'd ask if it were me. And I don't want to put that kind of finality on anyone. What you and I have, or don't have, it's between you and me. We've been avoiding this showdown for the entire nine years we've been divorced. We've had an ongoing thing. One that we clearly still haven't resolved. So…we're finally talking about it. We need to resolve it. However that happens, I have no more idea than you do, but at least we're acknowledging the need. And the fact that we both want a solution. We just don't have it yet. And I don't want the final moment to be our baby's conception."

"But it can be after tonight?"

She moved on him then, reaching her hand down between her legs to rub him through his pants, ready to just get them off.

"If it has to be," she said. She knew what she was saying. Meant it.

"But let's make it really good, okay? So if it has

to be the last time, we went out with a joining that blew us both away?"

Raising his hands, he started to softly roll her nipples between his fingers.

She lifted her body enough to undo his fly and release his penis, and then, with both hands, slid her jeans down as far as she could get them. Far enough that she could straddle him.

"Wait." He said the words as she was already shoving her hand beneath his butt to find his wallet. The condom was out and on while he was still busy at her breasts, keeping those shards of fire shooting down to her crotch.

And then she slid home, taking all of him, in all of her, and just didn't care in those seconds about right and wrong.

She was where she belonged for that moment. And moved with a ferociousness to prove it.

They came almost immediately, one right after the other. Her first, and then, her pulsing around him setting him off.

When they were done, she started to move, slowly, not at all eager to move on to the next phase of whatever future awaited her.

"Oh, no," Martin said, holding her in place. "You said it had to blow us away." He was totally serious, his voice gravelly. "And while that was better than average, it's nowhere near what we can do," he continued, moving inside her again. "I want the night, Liv. All of it. Can you give that to me?"

She'd always struggled to deny him anything he asked. That night she didn't even have to try. "I want the night, too," she told him. "Show me your stuff, sir."

The nickname slipped out. One she'd hit him with the first night he asked her out. He'd been far more concerned about their age difference than she had, and she'd teased him with the moniker.

She hadn't called him that in years.

Afraid that she'd offended, she bent to kiss him and saw a glisten of emotion clouding his eyes. "Only you have a way of calling me that that turns me on," he told her, flipping them over, ridding them both of their pants and changing his condom for a new one as he did so.

Naked on top of her he moved his penis inside her slowly, kissing her, running his hands through her hair. She opened her eyes to see the awe in his as he watched her.

And once again, she was lost.

He couldn't hold on to her. Martin knew that. Olivia was too vibrant. Too vital. She had too much to do with her life to be trapped in his world of fund-raising and parties and business deals. He was dedicated to doing good work with his fortune, but he needed to enjoy the world, too. She needed to save it first. He kept going by getting the most out of every day of his life. Enjoying every day. She kept going by working her way through every day. Whether she was at work or not. Always thinking of others, serving others. Her focus on helping others to the exclusion of having fun or doing for herself seemed to be the way she prevented herself from being consumed by the pain.

Survival for him meant finding the joy so he didn't get pulled under by the losses. She seemed to find the strength to keep going by paying penance every single day for something that hadn't been her fault.

After incredible lovemaking Thanksgiving night, his ex-wife had once again left his bed in the early hours of the morning, refusing to share even a cup of coffee with him—giving new meaning to the term Black Friday.

They'd texted as he'd traveled over the couple of weeks that had followed. Innocuous messages that left him needing more.

At least that was what he told himself as the weeks between Thanksgiving and Christmas passed. As usual he kept busy, more so with the holidays upon them. While some of his business meetings slowed down, the social invitations tripled and he had days where he was going from the moment he rose at dawn until he fell into bed after midnight, exhausted enough to sleep.

At least for a few hours. And when he awoke and lay there alone with thoughts of Olivia and the baby creeping in, he'd get up and get going. At work in his home office. For a walk on the beach. Or he'd just head into Fishnet headquarters. He'd lived enough years to know how to deal with life.

Or he'd missed the boat and wasn't ever going to get it.

He wasn't always sure which.

More and more he was warming up to the idea of him and Olivia continuing on as they had been since their divorce, which mostly worked for them over the past nine years, and giving up on his idea of a life partner. He could very likely have a child to consider in a few months and there was no way he could turn his back on that. Which meant he couldn't cut Olivia out of his life.

And it was pretty clear neither of them was going to be able to trust that one or the other would be strong enough to keep their hands off each other in perpetuity.

After Thanksgiving night, and the way it stayed with him, he was beginning to suspect that, baby or not, he'd never get Olivia out of his system. Which meant that he had to give up on the goal of finding his life partner. He certainly wasn't going to ask a potential wife to share her rightful place with another woman.

Nor did he want to share the coming baby with

another woman. Only he and Olivia knew what that
child meant to them. Only the two of them shared
the pain of having lost Lily together.

He'd learned as a kid that you didn't always get
what you wanted. Just as he'd learned to lead with
his heart, always look for the good and to work hard
for whatever it was he wanted.

His parents had taught him how to love uncondi-
tionally, and how to do without material things. They
just hadn't shown him how to give up.

Olivia hadn't said where she was at with any of
it. As usual, she wasn't saying much of anything. He
knew she was in touch with Beth regularly, though he
didn't know if that meant daily, weekly or some other
time frame. And he knew that Beth was still pregnant.

As Christmas approached, they were closing in on
two of the three critical months. Getting closer to the
chance that there was really going to be a baby born
as a combination of his and Olivia's genetic pools. A
sister or brother to Lily. He had no idea how he felt
about that. Fiercely protective. Needing everything to
be okay. And not wanting anything to change. How
could Lily have a brother or sister when she couldn't
meet him or her? And what about the sibling born
after Lily's death never knowing Lily?

The Applegates had invited them for Christmas
dinner. Sylvia had also been included in the invitation but had again declined, opting to spend the
latter part of the day with her same friend who'd re-

cently lost a spouse. She and Olivia would be spending Christmas Eve and Christmas morning together. They hadn't invited him.

Not that he'd expected them to do so. He'd expected to be in Italy for the holiday, in Rome for Christmas Eve service, and then with friends on a yacht in the Mediterranean. Old techie buddies who, collectively, donated more than half a million dollars a year to Fishnet. And whose party grew exponentially if they could say he was a guest.

But with the ultrasound scheduled for the morning of December 24, one day shy of two months from conception, there was no way he could leave the country. If there was anything at all of concern in that film, he had to be available to Olivia. Available for his child.

And no way he was sending her to the Applegates' alone, either. She'd be fine, he was sure. It was him who couldn't bear to think of her feeling in any way like an outsider, the only one present who was not an immediate member of the close-knit family, on Christmas Day.

Because he was always traveling he hadn't decorated for the holiday in years—not since he and Olivia had split—but came home a few days before Christmas to find Tammy, his housekeeper, and Barbara, his administrative assistant, collaborating together to put holiday cheer in his large, luxurious and suddenly lonely-feeling condo.

The curious loneliness was only because he'd had

to cancel all of his holiday plans. He got that. Still, it was nice to have some festivity around. Warmed the place up a bit.

And because he was in town, he waited until two days before Christmas to do his own shopping. He only bought for Barbara and Tammy and their families. Barbara did the rest of any gift buying for him. And to him shopping meant going to the upscale store he frequented once a year, picking out items and paying to have them gift wrapped and delivered. Still it was nice to do so while the world around him was bustling with cheer and last-minute chaotic energy. He was usually ensconced in massive holiday plans by that point of the year. Not out in the middle of the frenzy.

He and Olivia hadn't exchanged gifts—by mutual decision—since the year they'd divorced. This year would be no different.

He was just on his way out of the store when he passed by a jewelry display. Set up on a backdrop of black velvet was an exquisite eighteen-karat-gold flat heart. Flowing out of the right side of the top of the heart was a Madonna figure curved around the left side with a smaller, flowing baby. It stopped him in his tracks. The piece was delicate. And, as he stood there, it seemed to exude strength beyond his understanding. And something more. It was so fragile, and yet…unbreakable, too.

He had to have it. There was no internal discussion, no monologue, dialogue or even thought that went into the decision. He stepped up to the counter, and when a saleswoman immediately approached, he asked no questions, didn't even ask to touch the piece, before putting his card down on the glass.

He didn't request gift wrapping or delivery, either.

Two short minutes later, with the velvet box a small bulge in the front pocket of his pants, he walked out of the store.

Sylvia had urged that they do Christmas at Olivia's condo that year again. Olivia didn't argue but felt bad that her mom didn't get to have her home filled with the holiday cheer. On Wednesday evening, two days before Christmas, and the day before Beth's first ultrasound, they were busy unpacking decorations and putting them on the tree Olivia had purchased and brought home that afternoon. She always waited until the last days the trees were on the lot, telling herself that she was giving days of love to one that would have ended up in a chipper instead of spreading holiday cheer. Instead, she usually ended up with a tree that dropped needles everywhere just getting it into the condo.

That evening was no different and Sylvia, who'd definitely grown used to her routine, already had the vacuum out and running while Olivia got the bins of ornaments out from Christmas storage underneath the stairwell.

As was tradition, they'd both dressed in jeans

and Christmas sweaters. And Sylvia's Crock-Pot of homemade grape jelly meatballs was already plugged in in the kitchen. The cheese and crackers and veggies they'd eat with it were prepared on trays.

Her mother had told her the first year they'd celebrated Christmas together, the first year she'd been divorced, that she wanted for them to have their own family traditions, separate and apart from what either of them had known being raised by Olivia's grandmother. Would there be brand-new traditions the next time they celebrated Christmas? Ones to enjoy with a new baby who'd just be learning to crawl?

She could let herself get a brief glimpse, and then her mind shut off. It was too soon to let herself fall too far in.

And so it was. Christmas carols played loudly over the sound system, scents of dinner cooking filled the air and there was a bowl of individually wrapped holiday chocolates on the coffee table.

It felt like home. Like tradition. And yet, for the first time in several years, Olivia didn't feel complete.

Because of the appointment looming the next morning. She knew her unease stemmed from the unknown, from what they might or might not find in Beth's stomach.

If a Christmas miracle existed for her, there'd be a heartbeat. It was all she could think about. "Alexa, please play Kelly Clarkson's 'Heartbeat Song.'

"What time do you want me to pick you up in the morning for the appointment?" she asked Sylvia when her mother pushed the vacuum to the corner and took a lid off the bin of lights they'd string on the tree. The lights were always first, and they did them together, one on each side of the tree, passing them back and forth.

"Is Martin going to be there?"

Her mother hadn't asked up to that point. She hadn't said. Had hoped it wasn't going to come up.

"Yes."

"Then I'm going to go ahead into work. The holidays are such a stressful time to so many and the smallest thing can trigger an episode," she said, handing Olivia the end of the first string of lights. Sylvia typically worked long hours over the holidays. Her clients with PTSD did tend to have more issues over the holidays. Olivia had to work on Christmas Day sometimes; it all came with the profession.

But...

Starting the lights at the top, she reached up and secured the end, wrapped it as far as she easily could from her position and passed the strand. "You were planning to come until I said Martin was going to be there."

Sylvia wound and passed back. "I was hoping he was coming and was planning to cancel tomorrow morning's second appointment to go with you if he wasn't driving down."

The explanation was feasible, and Olivia was done skirting the issue. There were just too many of them piling up on her. She wrapped. Waited. Wrapped again. And when it was time to plug the second strand into the first, she held it instead, looking at her mother.

"You think I'm wrong to include him," she said. "You think I'm getting into something that can only hurt all of us at some point. That I'm digressing…"

The stunned look on Sylvia's face stopped her tirade. "I don't think any of that," she said, her shoulder-length dark hair bobbing with every word.

"It's obvious you don't want to be around him," she persisted. "Which means you disapprove."

"Olivia—"

The placating tone had her interrupting. "You never liked me with him, and you were proven right. I get it. But he's the baby's father, whether we would choose the situation or not."

She said "we." As though she wouldn't choose for her baby's father to be Martin. And Olivia felt immediately horrible. As though she was going to be cursed.

Truth was, she couldn't imagine any other man she'd ever want to father her child. Martin was the most decent, kind and giving man she'd ever met. The smartest. Most responsible. And sexiest, too, not that she was going to share that last with her mother.

With only sixteen years' age difference between

her and Sylvia, and both having been raised by the same woman, they were sometimes as much sisters or friends as mother and daughter, but still…

"I told you before… I was wrong in some of my assumptions where he was concerned," Sylvia said slowly, reaching for the lights and plugging the end into the strand already on the tree. She wrapped and handed the strand to Olivia. "I admire the heck out of what he's done with his life," Sylvia continued, her voice slightly muffled by the tree between them. "And I can't help but be aware of how he's remained a part of your life for the nine years since your divorce."

Sylvia knew they'd been in touch. She had no idea they'd been having occasional sex for every one of those nine years. Olivia wound and passed.

"I also can't help being aware that I might have screwed up nine years ago."

Olivia took the strand again and stepped to the right until she could look at her mother. "What do you mean?"

Taking the lights from Olivia's hand, Sylvia finished wrapping the tree. Plugged the bottom cord into the cord that they'd bought years before that plugged into the wall and provided a step on-and-off button. She stepped and the tree came to life with beautiful, sparkling color.

"Come, sit," she said, with such authority Olivia felt as though her mother had just told her what to do.

And because she'd spent so much of her life

wanting just that—her own mother to be around, teaching her what to do, what to say, how to handle situations—she did as she was told. For so long, she'd been handling life alone, refusing to let herself need anyone to complete her like she'd needed Martin and Lily. Truth was, human beings weren't meant to be completely alone.

They were meant to coexist. To make their own choices, keeping others needs in mind. To be kind and aware.

And at that moment, she was aware that she was very likely going to be a mother.

And needed her own mother, too.

Chapter Sixteen

"You know all I've ever wanted is to be a good mother to you," Sylvia said, her gaze dead serious as she sat beside Olivia on the couch.

Olivia nodded, not at all sure where the conversation was going. Not comfortable, at all, either. She and Sylvia, they shied away from talking about some things. Like the way Olivia had grown up well loved but feeling abandoned at the same time.

"I know that you've always thought my choice to leave you with your grandmother, and finish high school living with my friend's family, and only seeing my mom when you didn't know I was around, was selfish on my part. I kind of got off scot-free, right? I made a mistake, got pregnant, had the child and then went on with my life, leaving all the responsibility, the accountability, behind."

Olivia didn't say a word. Sylvia was expressing things Olivia had told her years before. She couldn't very well deny their truth.

"I thought when Lily was born, you'd understand more," Sylvia said. "The unconditional love a parent feels for a child sometimes means you have to sacrifice your own heart and soul for that of your child. I was sixteen when you were born, Liv. A young, naive, vulnerable teen who'd thought I was loved and adored but had been taken advantage of. My mom, she was the best. She never blamed me or pointed fingers. She helped me find my strength in it all. To learn from it all and make more of my life because of it.

"But I wanted only what was best for you. From the second you were born. It killed me, almost literally, to walk away. Not to hold you, smell your sweet skin, hear your laughter and watch you grow...but it was the best thing for you. Having me around, confusing the issue as to who your parent was, who you should mind, who you should run to when you were hurting or scared...having me around and then leaving for college...or having me skip college and have no career with which to support you... In any case, it wasn't really left up to me. The only way Mom would take you was if I signed over guardianship and stayed out of your life."

She'd heard it all before, of course. The week she'd turned eighteen and her grandmother had decided it was time the two met.

They'd met two more times after that, at her grandmother's insistence, and then the week her grandmother died, her mother had pushed for more and, grieving, Olivia had opened her heart a bit more.

Olivia had already been seeing Martin.

"I was so desperate to be a good mother to you, to show you that I would be there for you, that I fear I made a grave error," Sylvia was saying now. Reminding Olivia that the conversation had started with the idea that Sylvia had made a mistake. And that it somehow had to do with Martin.

"After Lily died, you were so broken, Liv. So lost. I was like a mama bear, ready to do whatever it took to ease your pain. To help you recover…"

She remembered. There'd been a night or two when the darkness had consumed her and only pain seemed real, and then Sylvia had suddenly appeared in her room, with a soft touch, no words, just… there… She was pretty sure Sylvia had saved her life. She was certain her mother had saved her sanity. Which was how they'd become so close.

"The thing is, as I look back, I fear that it was about me then, too. I was so determined to be a good mom that I didn't step back and let you and Martin find your way together. Instead, I took over you and left him to deal with his grief on his own."

It hadn't been exactly that way, of course. She and Martin had spent weeks in that house in LA after Lily died. Arguing. Needing. Unable to provide. But Olivia could understand her mother's point.

"If I hadn't been there, so determined to hold you up, you and Martin would have turned to each other more."

Thinking back, Olivia could see some truth in her mother's words. Some.

"He didn't need me, Mom. Martin has never needed me."

And she hadn't realized how much that hurt, or even how significant a problem it had been for her until recently when, for the first time in their relationship, she'd suddenly felt, for a minute or two, that she could help him.

"Maybe he needed you and didn't get a chance to let you see that because I was so protective of you. Maybe he needed you and I was so busy making you take care of yourself, I didn't let you take care of him."

She didn't know what to say. Couldn't really argue her mother's point, because...well, there might have been some truth in it.

Ultimately, it changed nothing. She and Martin were still too opposite, wanting different things out of life, defining happiness differently, and yet... Sylvia's perspective made a difference.

"Is that why you won't go with us to the Applegates' on Friday?" she asked. "Because I think you should. If this baby makes it...you're going to be a grandmother and—"

With her hand on Olivia's, Sylvia silenced her. "I'll be the best damned grandmother any baby could hope to have, sweetie, but right now, I have to be the best mom I can be. And that means being here for you, putting you first, always, and stepping back when that means allowing you to have the best life you can have."

The words rang too true of her childhood. And yet…how did Sylvia know what would have been best for her then? She'd been a kid herself.

"Are you abandoning me again?" she asked, half joking. But not entirely.

"Never." Sylvia's eyes filled with tears. "You are always first with me, Olivia. Never doubt that. No matter what. You and what you need come first with me. As Lily did with you. And—" her mother's gaze deepened "—as this new baby will for you. It's time for you to allow your heart to open up to all of the possibilities that life is offering."

She was open. As open as she could be. She hadn't taken the morning-after pill. She'd asked for the embryo transfer. And she'd had sex with Martin again.

But, just like her mother getting pregnant at sixteen, and Olivia growing up feeling abandoned, just like having a uterus that had failed to properly nourish her baby, and having a beautiful, precious daughter who'd suffered and died, having infant patients who died, there were some things in life that weren't perfect. There were some things you just couldn't fix.

What in the hell was he going to do with a Madonna and child pendant?

Martin had pulled it out of his pocket as soon as he

was in his vehicle. Locking it in the glove box. And then went for it again when he got home—taking it into his bedroom, dropping it into the nightstand drawer.

He never should have bought it. Wasn't sure what had possessed him to do so.

A mother and child. Yeah, Olivia and…Lily? Olivia and the new baby?

What did it matter? They didn't exchange gifts.

But he wasn't planning to take it back, either.

Most of that evening he returned business calls from overseas. Made plans for the new year. Turned down an invitation from Victoria when she called to ask if he wanted to meet for drinks.

Telling her no hadn't been easy, but he felt so much better after he'd done so—effectively, in his mind, closing the door on future relationships for himself—that he went into the shower and then had an early night. Even if he was just watching television, he could rest.

Was feeling ready to do so.

He had to be in Marie Cove early, was picking Olivia up at home so they could drive to the ultrasound together. He'd never been to the clinic and hadn't wanted her to be alone. Hopefully the appointment would turn out well. There was no reason to think that it wouldn't. No sign that anything could be wrong.

But just in case, he didn't want Olivia to have to drive if they got bad news.

If there was no heartbeat.

When Olivia texted after ten on Wednesday night, suggesting that she and Martin meet at the Parent Portal instead of her place the next morning, he got disgruntled all over again.

She was pushing him away again. Keeping him firmly on the outside of any emotional needs she might have. Building the damned wall ever higher.

The pendant in the drawer next to him mocked him. When had he become such a sentimental old fool?

Even if all went well—and he fully suspected it would—she'd have to feel some fallback from the fact that it would be Beth, not herself, on that table, her insides projected to the monitor. Watching her baby move in another woman.

And there could be residual memories of her own time having that particular test.

With Lily.

Lying naked except for a pair of cotton sleep shorts in the bed he'd shared with her the last time they'd seen one another, he started to text her back and, leaving a half-typed message sitting on his screen, hit Call instead.

"Why the change of plans?" he asked as soon as she picked up. He wasn't behaving well. Heard the cranky tone in his voice. Knew he didn't want to fight with her.

And waited.

"Because I have to work tomorrow," she said. "A schedule change. I have a new patient that I'm following closely. The next twenty-four hours are critical and I switched with another doctor so that I could be there."

It didn't have to happen that way. Doctors covered for each other on a regular basis.

"Last I knew you wanted the ultrasound scheduled on your day off…" Just in case, he'd surmised.

"Yes. But, you know, maybe it's better this way. I won't have time to wallow in my own sauce if I'm at work. I'm at my best there, and that's what everyone needs from me right now. To be at my best."

It was a curious statement, the fact that she'd shared the thought even more so.

"Who's everyone?" He turned off the bedside light and lay there facing the wall of windows looking out over the city with the darkness of the ocean broken by bobbing pieces of light beyond.

"You. The potential baby. My mom. Beth… Just everyone."

She'd named him first. He couldn't make too much of it.

And it mattered.

"Why do you think I need you at your best?"

She didn't have a quick comeback. He waited through her pause.

"I don't. Not you necessarily. Just…our situation. It's challenging. There are no easy answers. We're trying to figure out what to do and I need to give it my best. If this baby matures, it will need me to have given it my best."

Propping pillows up behind him, he wished she was there in the room with him. That he could look in her eyes. Reach for her—not sexually at the moment—just to talk.

Because suddenly she *was* talking. Not just about their situation, but about herself in dealing with it. The distinction might be slight, but it seemed huge.

"I never needed you to be your best, Liv. I just needed you to let me see you."

"You didn't *need* me at all. You needed to take care of me, maybe. And you did see me."

"In the beginning, maybe. When things got rough, even before Lily was born, you were already building up walls to shut me out. Which made me push harder until it felt like I was suffocating you. So, I backed off, gave you your space, and that didn't work, either. It just gave you a chance to strengthen the walls."

"You never suffocated me, Martin. But your constant need to fix things started to make me feel like I couldn't do things for myself. I started to feel less and less capable. Like I needed you for everything. But you didn't need me at all. It was like our relationship was all about you taking care of me."

She'd said twice in less than five minutes that he hadn't needed her. He didn't compute that. Couldn't figure out where she was even coming from with that one. But the rest, his need to fix things…he felt the sting of truth in her words.

"I'm a guy who sets a goal and then gives all my energy into achieving that goal," he said slowly. "When I married you, I promised to have your back for the rest of my life, to do everything in my power to make you happy. That was my goal…and yet, no matter how hard I tried, how many ways I tried, I couldn't achieve that goal."

"My happiness was never your responsibility," she told him. "In the first place, a person has to choose to be happy, to allow the good feeling in, to acknowledge it when it's there, notice it, look for it. And in the second place, we got pregnant so quickly, and then to find out that she hadn't grown as she should have done… That was completely outside of your control."

"But having me around should have helped. It didn't."

Her pause was longer and the silence rang like a death knell on any future they might try to build together. Even a parental one.

She cleared her throat and he sat up. Was she crying? Oh God, the last thing he'd wanted was to make her cry.

"I, uh, had kind of an odd conversation with Sylvia tonight." Her words weren't at all what he'd expected; her voice was filled with questions…but no tears.

"Odd how?"

"Well, in the first place, she doesn't dislike you."

"I never thought she did. She just didn't want me around you. And looking back, I don't blame her," he said, words he'd held for years breaking free. Less than two months ago they'd said they were never going to see each other again. There was nothing to lose by not holding back.

Instead of trying to hold on, they'd hit rock bottom, and could only go up from there.

Had to find a way to go up if their baby gestated.

Or maybe he just had to let go. "I never should have married you, Liv." He told her what he'd known for a while. "I should have left you to grow up a bit more and find a man your own age. Or, at the very least, waited a lot longer before I asked you to marry me. Instead, I cashed in on the intensity of our feelings for each other and fast-tracked you to my time frame. I was in my thirties, needing to start a family, and I put that on you immediately, rather than letting you be a college student, giving you time to find your way in the world first. I knew the way and thought I could teach you. What I didn't realize was that we each had to find our own way."

He heard a sound, movement of some kind. Knew she was there. "Wow." The one word came a good thirty seconds after he'd quit talking.

"Um, that's...not where I was going...at all."

He'd surprised her. Good to know he still could, he supposed. And knew that he was a sitting duck, right there in his own bed, waiting for her to put him out of his misery. To agree with him.

But maybe that's where this had all been leading. A place where they could accept they'd made a mistake and figure out how to create a future where they could be friends. Or something. For the baby's sake.

If there came to be one.

The ultrasound the next day…if there was a heartbeat…if measurements were in normal range… they were going to have to start planning.

To find the answers.

The baby wasn't going to wait around for its parents to figure out what to do.

"I really don't know what to do with all of that," Olivia said slowly. "I can argue part of it… I was an adult, Martin. I knew my own mind. Even in that whole thing you just said, you talked as though I was a child and you were an adult. I certainly wasn't the only twenty-year-old getting pregnant. Women a lot younger than me have babies and are great moms.

"That said, there might be some truth to you rushing me. I've always believed you didn't need me. Have always felt that you didn't. But maybe, if I'd been a little older…maybe I was too young, too caught up in my own stuff, to be a proper wife to you. The guys I was used to just put whatever was on their minds out there. But you, with your maturity, you'd already learned to take life as it came…which was one of the things that most attracted me to you to begin with."

Interesting. More than interesting. For a second there the knot in his gut loosened.

"I also think it was just fate," she said next, speaking softly. He wondered if she was in bed. Looking out her window as he was looking out his.

Funny how they both had bedrooms with full window views, just like their home when they'd been married.

"I was young, yes, but what happened with Lily... Age wasn't going to make that pain any less unbearable."

"Nope." He had to agree. "It didn't."

"Sylvia was talking about all of that tonight," Olivia said next, reminding him that she'd started out telling him her mother didn't dislike him.

And wondered why her mother had raised the subject. Because Olivia had been having a hard moment as she faced the ultrasound, faced the possibility that there'd be no heartbeat, not enough growth, no viable pregnancy, just one that had not yet naturally aborted itself?

"She thinks she's partially responsible for our divorce. She thinks that if she hadn't swooped in to be a great mother to me, you and I might have turned to each other more."

He couldn't tell if Olivia agreed, or not.

And wasn't sure he did. For his part, sure, he'd have liked to have had his wife to himself. But Liv had been so young, and so devastated...

"You needed her," he admitted. "You needed a woman who understood. I wasn't ever going to get what it felt like to carry a baby inside my body and then have to watch it die."

He'd tried so hard to understand. And just hadn't.

"I didn't get why you blamed yourself," he told her now. "I still don't. It's like telling someone who's born blind that it's their fault they can't see."

"A mother instinctively needs to know she can keep her child safe…" Olivia's tone had weakened. "I failed to do that in the most elemental way. I've been told I'm incapable of doing it. It's a feeling that cuts to the core. Logic holds no bearing on it."

"And so, tomorrow…when you watch your baby move inside another woman's body…are you going to be okay with that?"

She laughed, and gulped, too. "If there's a baby moving in there, I don't care if it's inside the pope, I'm going to be okay with it," she said. And then sniffed. "And no, of course not," she added softly, and that time he heard tears in her voice. "How can I be? Knowing that I can't gestate my own child? That someone else is going to feel it grow? And kick. Knowing that my baby is going to bond so intimately with another woman before it even meets me?"

That. That's what he needed. *Her.* In all her rawness.

"And that's how it feels to be a father," he said, just making the connection himself, remembering how cut off he felt from the bond between Lily and Olivia during her pregnancy. "So, tomorrow, we'll be in it together."

Maybe it wouldn't help. There was no way to fix her uterus, to allow her to carry her own child. He couldn't do it. No one could. But he could be there.

Understanding.

And maybe, by just standing next to each other through what was to come, even without all the answers, they could find a way to become friends.

Chapter Seventeen

Surprisingly, the call with Martin the night before seemed to have put Olivia in a place better suited to handling the prospect of the ultrasound Thursday morning.

Christmas Eve day.

While traffic had been bustling on the streets of Marie Cove that morning, with last-minute shopping and holiday errands quickly reaching critical deadline stage, the Parent Portal was unusually quiet. Beth's car was the only one in the patient parking lot when she pulled in.

Olivia wore black casual pants and a long-sleeved red top with a smiling snowman emblazoned on the front. She was debating whether she should wait for Martin or go in and talk to Beth when she saw his vehicle pull into the lot.

For a split second, she had a vision of a young group of boys piling out of the second and third seats, leaving snack bags and crumbs behind them, and then shook the idea away. She'd long since realized the danger of creating fantasies. No way would she and Martin ever be that family.

She waited for him, though, wishing her hair were down, a blanket of sorts, instead of in the work bun that left her so fully exposed. She wanted to thank him for their conversation the night before. To let him know that it had helped.

And then, when he joined her, didn't do it.

It was one thing to let down her emotional guard with him when they were on the phone. And quite another, apparently, when his tall frame was flesh and blood beside her, looking all sexy and success-ful in a dark suit and red tie.

"It's not a formal occasion," she said, realizing even as she did so that her nervousness was showing.

"Since you're working, I filled my schedule for the day," he told her. He'd met her gaze once. She'd looked away first.

And that seemed to set the tone. There'd be no in-timacy between them during the appointment ahead. No opening of emotional wells.

Too much risk of an overflow that could drown them.

Drown her.

Beth had already been called back to prepare for the ultrasound by the time they were inside. Since the clinic wasn't open for other patients that day, only a receptionist, the ultrasound technician and Beth's clinic doctor, Cheryl Miller, were there.

And Christine… She came through the inner door

to the reception area before the woman who'd greeted them had even finished her first sentence.

Making a beeline for Olivia, the pregnant woman hugged her just when Olivia started to feel weak in the knees. "You've got this, my friend," Christine said, pulling back, looking Olivia in the eye. "Just like you told me, you want to do this."

You want to do this. They were the words she'd said to Christine when her friend had been telling herself that she couldn't possibly be a surrogate mother to a baby as a favor to a man who'd lost his wife—the baby's biological mother.

It had been a hard choice. A seemingly impossible one. But she'd known Christine needed to try.

Smiling, Olivia nodded, and Martin stepped forward. "Christine, this is Martin," she said, watching for her friend's first impression of the man she'd been hearing about for years but never met.

"Good to meet you." Christine held out her hand, shook Martin's and smiled. "Good to know you aren't a ghost."

"Excuse me?" Martin cocked his head in that way he had when he was trying to size up a situation.

"I've been hearing about you for years," the clinic owner said. "It's good to finally meet you."

Martin nodded, said something pleasant. Olivia wasn't sure what exactly as the ultrasound technician stood in the doorway. "We're ready," she said.

Oh God. They were ready.

Olivia wasn't. She'd thought she was. She'd had strength from the moment she opened her eyes that morning.

Christine squeezed her hand. And then Martin took ahold of it and didn't let go. "Let's go be parents," he said to her. "Because no matter what happens next, we made a viable embryo, and you did everything you could to keep it safe."

If she hadn't already been in love with him, she'd have fallen hard in that moment.

Didn't matter that they'd failed at marriage. And at being divorced. Didn't matter that they couldn't even figure out how to be friends.

All that mattered was that he was there.

If ever there were a time when he felt like a fraud, it was as Martin walked back to the ultrasound room with Olivia, holding her hand like they were a couple.

Like he had a right to do so.

The woman who'd hugged his wife had disappeared in another direction. He'd heard of her, of course, recently, when Olivia had talked about the embryo transfer. He'd had no idea the two were close friends.

And had been for years apparently, based on the fact that Christine knew all about him.

He knew nothing about her. Except that she was clearly pregnant.

And that she figured into Olivia's confidences, had her trust, in a way Martin never had.

Before he could process any further, they were shown into a shadowy room with Beth lying on a padded table, watching them enter. She reached out a hand to Olivia, who let go of Martin to go stand by the other woman's side. Beth's stomach was exposed from her ribs to her pelvis, with her leggings and T-shirt pushed down and up to accommodate the test.

He'd been to several ultrasounds before—they'd had them weekly toward the end of Olivia's pregnancy with Lily—but technology had changed a lot in ten years.

As he well knew. Technology was his field.

Ultrasounds and babies and women who had them were not.

"You ready?" Beth asked Olivia, her brows drawn in concern, but a smile on her face. Their surrogate wiggled her feet, like she was revving up to run a race.

"I'm ready," Olivia told her. As the technician began to rub the cold gel on Beth's belly, Martin kept his eyes on Olivia. The stark, emotionless expression on her face. The doctor had entered the room and he envied her that.

He had no bedside manner upon which to pull. He was Martin Wainwright, a lover of most people, no matter what room he was in.

But lover only to one. For the past while. Maybe forever.

In that moment it mattered.

"Okay, here we go. If you watch up here…" The technician, a youngish woman, thirty or so, with long dark hair tied back in a ponytail and wearing light blue scrubs, pointed to a large monitor turned so that they could all see it. And then lowered her probe to Beth's skin.

He glanced at the screen long enough to see clear white fuzz, and then focused on Olivia. Her lips were pinched, but she appeared to be the essence of calm. Until he saw the whites of her fingertips as she held Beth's hand.

The technician lifted the probe, put it back down, moved it around. He could follow the motions with peripheral vision as he continued to watch his ex-wife. He was there for her. Ready to step up and take hold if she lost her composure.

And knowing that he had to let her get through the next moments in her own way. To cope on her own.

Clearly the technician was having trouble finding anything to land on.

As though there was no fetus growing there.

No one said a word. The silence was about to kill him. He could hardly breathe. This couldn't be happening. Not to Olivia. Not to him.

Not again.

Maybe it hadn't been an issue with her uterus, after all. Maybe it had been his sperm. And because of him she'd be going through hell a second time.

And so would he.

He'd been so sure that everything would be okay. So worried about how to fit being a father into his life.

What in the hell had he done?

He should have been celebrating from the second Olivia had told him she'd saved their embryo. That was his child they were trying to find in there.

Find it! His mind said the words forcefully. And then hollered them. *Damn it! Find it!*

On a second pass, there was still nothing. On the third, lower on Beth's stomach, the handheld device found enough to stop, hover and then start a slow circular motion in the same area.

"There," the technician said. And stopped, writing something down. She did the same thing another time. And another. Taking measurements? He hoped.

He had no way of knowing if she was finding a two-month gestated fetus or a sac that was going to miscarry. Beth was watching, her face serious, completely silent. And Olivia appeared to be frozen over there, staring at the screen.

No one was saying anything.

And there was a very clear absence of smiles in the room.

There was movement on the screen. He told himself that was a good thing. He just honestly had no idea if the movement was the baby or Beth's internal organs. If he looked hard, he could pretend he saw arms and legs, a head and torso, but in truth he saw various lighter and darker shadows that could really depict any number of things.

He wanted the longish darker outlined spot to be a torso. Kept going back to it. Over and over. Olivia's face, then that spot. He suddenly wanted that thing to be his baby's body more than he could remember wanting anything in his life.

He needed someone to say something. To ask something. To know something. But couldn't bear to be the bringer of bad answers into the room, fearing they'd pull out all the air, suffocate him.

"We can try to find a heartbeat," the technician said then. "But it's possible we won't be able to get it."

Martin fell back against the wall. There was no chair for him to collapse on. The news was bad. Obviously whatever Olivia had seen, whatever the technician had seen, hadn't been great if they weren't sure there was a heartbeat.

That blob could have been his baby's torso, but perhaps it hadn't grown enough. Because it had stopped growing?

Or was it just small? Maybe the baby could still be alive and just be small?

He stood up straight.

She'd said they could try for a heartbeat.

She wouldn't have said that if she'd been certain that the fetus was dead. No one would be that cruel.

And…they had a neonatologist in the room. Martin glanced at Olivia, needing to absorb her pain so he didn't feel any of his own. Hers he could handle.

She was watching him, her brow crunched, and held out her free hand to him. He could feel Beth's gaze on him as he moved closer but had eyes only for his ex-wife. Her gaze drew him.

Her need drew him.

As soon as their skin touched, he took a breath. And another. Only just realizing he'd been holding it. That the constriction of muscles in his chest had stopped air flow.

The technician had been pushing the probe around, doing whatever, he didn't know. He just watched Olivia and took strength from the times she glanced from the screen back to him.

He heard a sudden gurgling sound, like someone had sucked in, and steadied himself, watching only Olivia, keeping himself strong so that when she looked at him, she'd be able to feed off his strength. There was a second gurgle. Definitely not a heartbeat sound...

But then it came again, more of a slurp than a gurgle. And again. And again. And again.

In rhythm.

Olivia was crying. Beth was crying. The technician was crying.

And so was he.

They had a live fetus.

He was going to be a father.

Chapter Eighteen

"We have to talk." Olivia glanced at Martin as he murmured the words to her on the way out to the clinic's waiting room and exit to the parking lot.

With Beth and the doctor talking behind them, she nodded her agreement.

They both had recordings of the baby's heartbeat on their phones. Had digital copies of the ultrasound images there, too. They'd been in to see the doctor and heard that the fetus was measuring in the average percentile for two months' gestation, though Olivia had already read that for herself during the ultrasound. Just as she'd seen that everything else looked as normal as normal could get.

She had a healthy baby!

At two months.

Lily had appeared a bit small, but normal, too, during the first ultrasound.

And it was time to get off the treadmill they'd been running for too many years. Time to move forward.

Together or apart.

And not just for the baby, though definitely the pregnancy had become their catalyst.

They had a heartbeat!

She had no bill to take care of that day. No business to tend to. Christine had given her a tight hug as they'd come out of the ultrasound room on the way to see the doctor, and she'd already left. Olivia had thanked Beth so many times she'd probably come across like she was babbling. Had already confirmed the time for dinner the next day.

So there was nothing to do but walk out of the clinic with Martin.

And face their future.

"What are you doing for Christmas morning?" she asked him, as though she could buy herself just a few more minutes.

He shrugged. "Relaxing. I'm looking forward to it." He wasn't smiling, but there was something new about him. An energy. A sense of…purpose?

"Alone?" She tried to meet his gaze, but the sun was bright and he'd put on his shades. Pulling hers out of her purse, she did the same.

"I think so," he said. "I had a couple of brunch invitations, but… I'm just not feeling it." Cocking his head, he added, "We'll see. I can always change my mind."

"Come to my place."

Dumb words, she was sure of it. And left the invitation out there. They had a shared heartbeat. "Tonight, if you'd like," she continued. "I'm working until eight, so Sylvia's hanging with friends. She'll be over first thing in the morning with breakfast casserole."

He stopped. Turned until he was facing her. "You're inviting me to spend the night with you."

They'd had sex on Thanksgiving. One more time wouldn't make much difference. But that honestly wasn't her plan.

"We need to talk," she told him. "We can't keep putting it off."

She'd heard a heartbeat!

And the life she'd saved deserved a healthy, secure, consistent home environment.

Not a love affair.

His slow, serious nod put dread in her heart where she so desperately needed hope.

They made love first. As soon as Martin walked in the door of her condo, his overnight satchel still slung over his shoulder, he put an arm around Olivia and pulled her to him.

She'd recently showered. Her long hair smelled like roses and still had some damp strands. And she was wearing black cotton pajama pants and a pink-and-black long-sleeved T-shirt that matched. He knew the brand without even looking. From the time he'd known her, Olivia had only worn one brand of underwear, bras and pajamas.

Her lips met his openly, with hunger, and, dropping his bag, he pulled her completely into his arms, needing to devour her. To wipe out all thought of saying goodbye.

"This is the one thing we always got right," he murmured against her lips before picking her up and carrying her to the sectional couch in her living room. The furniture closest to where they were standing.

The Christmas lights were on in the otherwise dark room, giving the space a colorful, muted glow, and he memorized every inch of her skin as he undressed her. No matter where his life took him, he'd never hold in his arms a woman who affected him as Olivia did. Who was as beautiful to him as she was.

Who raised such a mixture of protectiveness and passion within him.

He'd failed her before. He'd known that for years. But throughout that day, after having seen her with Christine that morning, he'd finally realized exactly how he'd done so. He'd worshipped her. He just hadn't been a friend to her. He'd been her champion, her warrior, her protector—he hadn't been her partner.

And she hadn't been his, either.

Their lives existed in two different spheres.

They didn't speak just then—the words waiting to be said weren't lovemaking words. They both knew that. The choices waiting for them weren't going to be easy.

But he'd sensed, as soon as they'd walked out

of that ultrasound room with their recordings, that they both knew their time had come to make those choices.

They'd held on as long as they could.

And after he donned his condom, felt the pulsing of her pleasure and came inside her, he knew it was time to let her go.

"I sent a copy of the recording to Sylvia." Olivia broke the silence that had fallen over a room that felt sacred, the Christmas tree lights their only source of illumination. Martin, who was sitting on the opposite end of the couch from her, had put his pants and shirt back on, but the shirt was unbuttoned.

She stared at his chest hair as she spoke, remembering the feel of it beneath her cheek as she'd lain on him—so many times over the years.

"How does she feel about becoming a grandmother?" he asked, speaking as softly as she had. As though they could usher in the hard stuff in a way that wouldn't kill them.

"Good." Olivia smiled. "She called as soon as she heard the recording and was crying, too. She's thrilled…and…worried about me, too, I suppose. She says it's all part of being a mother."

And she was only just beginning to realize how very lucky she was to have a woman so wise in her life. She'd judged her mother harshly. Wrongly.

"I'm almost as old as she is."

Six years. That was the age difference between her mother and the father of her child. The idea didn't seem nearly as shocking to her as it had when she was in college and was just getting to know Sylvia. Maybe she'd grown used to it. Maybe she just didn't care so much anymore.

"Yeah," she said. "That used to bother me, you know. I knew that some of my friends, and my mother, thought you were too old for me and it bothered me even though I pretended it didn't. They saw the problems ahead of us. I didn't want to see them."

Another truth she'd never shared with him.

"It doesn't bother you anymore?"

Her shrug was the only honest answer she had. "Does it matter?"

"Maybe."

She thought about his question again. "It bothers me that you think you're too old to be a father." He wasn't. There were a lot of men having children in their forties. And fifties and sixties, too. But just because someone else did it didn't mean it was right for him.

"I am a father," he told her, looking her in the eye now. "It's not a question anymore."

Her heart started to pound. What was he telling her?

"I listened to that recording over and over today," he said.

"I did, too."

"It's a miracle."

She smiled. "I can hardly believe it yet. I think that's why I just kept playing it, any time I had a break. I just wish…"

She broke off…because from there, things got confusing. She wanted that baby more than anything. Would give her life for it.

And that heartbeat scared her to death.

"I wish we could be sure it'll be born healthy."

His nod was short. Succinct. She offered him a glass of wine. And, when he accepted, poured herself one, too, handed him his and sat back down on her end of the couch, her feet tucked up beneath the pajama pants she quickly put back on after they'd had sex.

"So what does the future look like to you?" she asked him as it became more and more clear to her that he wasn't going to just forge ahead with what he thought best, as he had in the past.

He shook his head. Shrugged.

Olivia sipped from her wine. Set it down on the end table beside her. Licked her lips. And sat up straight. "You're welcome to move in here, if you'd like," she said. She didn't see how it would work. They were more honest with each other than they'd ever been. Had both grown and learned. But the goals, the lifestyles, that had driven them apart still existed.

She also didn't see how they couldn't try.

"Something keeps pulling us back together," she dropped, almost defensively, into the silence.

He held his wineglass, staring as though it held the answer to a mathematical problem that had been eluding him—was *still* eluding him.

"I'm not suggesting we get married again," she continued to talk, feeling her way. "Just that we try to cohabitate again. You'd still live your life, travel, socialize, continue to meet all of your global business engagements. You'd just come here at night when you're in the state."

She didn't hate the idea.

Took hope when he didn't immediately discount it.

And lost it again when he set down his wineglass and stood.

His back to her, he faced the window that looked out over the city. "I can't go through it again."

She understood. Knew he was right to call her bluff.

"I don't think I can, either."

"We lost a baby!" He was yelling as he turned around. "She died!" He was angry. His eyes glistening. "We never even got to bring her home!" He spewed words filled with the unfairness of it all, his anguish obvious.

Mouth open, she sat there, completely shocked. He'd never...had all of that been bottled up inside him all those years? And she'd thought he'd been a wizard, dealing with the grief so much better than she could…

She watched him, like a train wreck happening right in front of her. Her chin started to tremble, and then her lower lip. There was nothing she could do to prevent the crash.

To save anyone from the pain that would follow.

"*Our* baby, Liv!" he said, turning back to the window. "She was our baby." His tone lowered. As did his head.

And she was filled with a strength she didn't know she had. Standing, with tears streaming down her face, she went to him, her fingertips tentative on his back at first. Touching gently. Small motions. Circular. With just the tips of her fingers. And soon, her hand. And the circle grew slowly bigger as she absorbed the force of his sobs into her palm, and into her heart.

She cried with him. Reliving those endless and too short months with sweet Lily. The look in her daughter's eyes when she'd walk in a room. The look in Martin's as he stood helplessly watching his family erode.

The small city skyline stretched before them, proof of a possibility that felt as though, for them, it had been snuffed out.

"Every time I think of us together…our family unit…is like a symbol of unbearable pain."

Her sudden intake of breath happened instinctively as he voiced what she'd been feeling since before their divorce.

"I loved her so much," she said. "More than I even knew it was possible to love someone."

Sliding an arm around her he kissed the top of her head. "I know," he said. "I loved her, too. Just as much. I'd have gladly given my life for her. But even my life wasn't enough to save her."

She wrapped her arms around him. Holding on as the tears slowly spent themselves. Time had no meaning as they stood there, facing the night—and the horrors of their past.

"I can't do it again, Liv." His voice was broken and he turned to face her, his features swollen. "I can't lose my family a second time."

She understood. Because she felt exactly the same.

They couldn't be that unit. It was a symbol of their worst nightmare.

"I can't move in with you, try again, fail and lose you a second time."

She got that, too, as tears trickled down her cheeks.

Chapter Nineteen

Martin offered to sleep on the couch. As ludicrous as it sounded, he had to respect the corner they'd turned. They could no longer find forgetfulness in each other's arms.

They'd brought their truth out into the open. Had let the pain that had severed their marriage slide in between them.

Olivia didn't even try to convince him otherwise.

If it hadn't been Christmas Eve, if they didn't have obligations the next day—responsibilities where the baby was concerned—he would have just left. Driven back to LA.

And done…he had no idea what. Couldn't come up with a scenario that appealed to him. He could always think of something that sounded good.

But not that night.

Instead, he lay on his ex-wife's couch and let the colorful lights on her tree drug him into a sense of nothingness. There was no peace for him that night.

Nothing that…kind.

But he didn't writhe in pain, either. He was spent.

Numb.

Eventually he dozed. And each time he awoke, the numbness remained. Thankful, he'd watch the lights and head off again.

He was adrift. Fitting nowhere. A part of nothing.

Christmas was about the birth of hope.

And he'd lost his.

Olivia called Sylvia first thing Christmas morning to warn her mother about her houseguest. To let Sylvia know that she and Martin had reached the same decision they'd reached before he'd known she'd been trying to save the life of their embryo.

They weren't going to see each other anymore. Not in any capacity.

They hadn't said so as yet, but she knew. He'd be sending financial support, setting up trust funds, keeping track of medical records, as was his right as a father, but he wasn't going to be requesting visitation or playing an active role in his child's life.

Where that left them in terms of guardianship in the event that anything happened to her, they hadn't said, but figured that communication challenge could be left for another day. Either Martin would step up to the plate, or he'd see to it that Sylvia was appointed custodial guardian. She trusted that with all her heart.

It was only after she'd been speaking to her mother for several minutes that she heard a sound in the background. A voice.

Most likely the television.

At seven o'clock on Christmas morning?

"Who's there?" she asked softly, hoping Martin would sleep until her mother got there. That he wouldn't try to make his escape.

"I'm here," Sylvia said. "And hold on, sweetie, I'll be there in ten. I've got the casserole out and ready to go. Everything else is already in my car."

Every year Sylvia showed up with a plethora of gifts. Making up for all of the years she couldn't watch Olivia open Christmas gifts, she'd once said. And because she loved shopping, and watching people open gifts, Olivia generally went overboard, too.

Pulling on black leggings and the thigh-length Christmas sweater she'd bought for a party the year before, and finishing with black ankle-length boots, she took a deep breath, smiled at herself in the mirror and headed out to the front room.

The presents she'd bought were in the front hall closet, ready to move under the tree—something she generally did before her mother arrived.

And there was Martin, still sleeping on the couch.

Relief hit her so hard tears sprang to her eyes. They'd really only had one good Christmas together. Had only exchanged gifts twice. Every year she saw things that made her think of him, things she knew he'd like, and every year she passed them by.

This year she hadn't. She'd purchased them. Wrapped them. And signed every one of them from the baby. She'd been living in fantasyland. She'd known it at the time.

And allowed herself the small comfort while she waited to find out if her baby was viable. To find out if Martin was going to be a part of their lives.

She'd taken a chance. Gambled.

And lost.

Still, as she put the coffee on and then pulled gifts out of the closet, quietly loading up the floor space under and around the tree, she carried his gifts out, too.

He was there. He had to have things to open.

She'd just carried in her last load, turned around to leave the room the way she'd come, avoiding the couch area, but unable to stop herself from sneaking one last peek at him, she saw him lying there, watching her.

His lids hung low, sleepy—the lazy look about him she'd always loved because it made him look so…accessible.

"You look beautiful." The husky voice encapsulated her with wanting, giving her delicious chills. And Sylvia would be walking in the door any minute, bringing holiday air in with her.

"Mom's on her way," she told him, moving slowly closer. "She knows you're here."

He didn't seem fazed either way. Nodded. And still she worried that he'd opt to leave rather than join them.

The thought of him driving back to LA all alone

on Christmas morning, to arrive at an empty condo and sit alone, broke her heart.

And yet...if that was the life that suited him, the life he needed...

"Can we...can we just put things aside for a few more hours?" she whispered, sitting on the edge of the couch in front of his midsection. She wanted to smooth the hair off his forehead, run her fingers through the slight showing of gray above his ears, but didn't touch him. "We have to be at the Applegates', anyway..."

Breaking off, filled with a new dread, she looked at him. "You're still going with me, aren't you?"

His nod brought a wave of happiness that probably wasn't warranted.

"And in answer to your other question, yes, we can put everything else aside for a few more hours." Sitting up, he wrapped an arm around her, kissed her and then stood up. "And if Sylvia's on the way, I need to get in the shower."

"Use mine," she told him as he picked up his bag, and when he did, when she could hear him moving around in the master suite, she went to set three place settings of Christmas china on the dining room table.

Sylvia not only had on leggings, her Christmas sweater and boots, also ankle-length, but she'd taken the time to put on full makeup, curl the ends of her shoulder-length dark hair and put on jewelry, too. Christmas tree earrings and a thick gold omega necklace.

"Wow, that's lovely," she said, touching the gold piece. "I've never seen it before."

"That's because it's new," Sylvia said, brushing by Olivia as she carried the casserole dish into the kitchen and put it in the oven Olivia had already warmed. Her mother was her usual Christmas morning chatty self as she carried in presents and placed them under the tree. Talking about a memory from her childhood, when it had been just her and her mother for Christmas, her father having died when she was a toddler, and they'd still had a pile of presents under the tree, music playing and magic in the air.

Taking her cue, Olivia found a station streaming Christmas music and set it to play over the home theater system. And listened for Martin to come down from upstairs.

"How about a mimosa?" Sylvia asked, carrying in a bottle of champagne and shutting the door behind her, signifying that it was her last trip out to the hall where the doorman had helped her gather her things. Olivia was specifically not allowed to help carry on Christmas morning. Sylvia had always insisted she could be her own Santa.

Mimosas were new for Christmas morning, but she wasn't opposed. Getting her finest crystal champagne flutes out of the cabinet—wedding gifts from long ago—she filled them with orange juice and bubbly, figuring the little bit of alcohol would be a good tension breaker as she finally heard Martin descending the stairs.

It had been years since her ex-husband and her mother had actually seen each other. She needed them to get along. Just for the one day.

She needed a real family Christmas memory to take with her into the future.

Turning from the counter with two drinks in her hand, intending to hand one to her mother and then reach for Martin's to give him as soon as he walked in the room, she noticed a fourth place setting at the table.

"What…"

She didn't get the sentence finished before there was a knock at the front door. She hadn't buzzed anyone in. Or put another name on the list with the doorman.

"I'll get that," Sylvia said, and left Olivia, open-mouthed, holding two glasses. Her mother had been running around like a bit of a nervous hen, but she'd put that down to Martin's presence in the condo.

"Who's here?" he asked, coming in from the opposite direction and taking the champagne flute she handed him.

"I think we're about to find out," she said, unable to stop herself from salivating for a second over his broad shoulders in the black sweater he was wearing, the damp hair and sexy stubble on his face.

"Merry Christmas," he said, tapping his glass to hers as her gaze went lower, noticing the fly of the black jeans he had on.

Martin in jeans had always been a sight that sent her heart thumping. He didn't wear them often, but when he did, it was like they were sewn together right on his body.

"Merry Christmas," she said back, barely tapping her glass to his before taking a huge gulp. There was more orange juice, and more champagne, and she had a feeling she was going to need them.

She heard her mother's voice, listened to see which girlfriend, or stray, she'd invited to Christmas breakfast without letting Olivia know, and froze when she heard the low tone of a male voice.

With a glance at Martin, and her glass firmly in hand, she headed toward the front room.

A man easily as tall as Martin, with white hair that curled at the collar of his red sweater, held bags in one hand, the other pulling back from under the tree, where he'd clearly just placed something.

She glanced at her mother.

"Sam..." Sylvia moved to the man's side and, as he straightened, hooked her arm through his. "I'd like you to meet my daughter, Olivia, and behind her is Martin. This is Sam," she said, her lip clearly trembling as her gaze implored Olivia.

For what, Olivia wasn't sure. Unless her mother was pleading silently with her to not be angry for springing a man on their Christmas morning.

Of course, she hadn't told Sylvia about Martin being there, either.

"I'm sorry for intruding," Sam, who was easily sixty, said, also appearing slightly apologetic as he glanced at Olivia and Martin, who'd come up to stand beside her. "I wasn't planning to come. The plan, actually, was for me to stay at Sylvia's for the morning…but—"

"Maybe we should sit," Sylvia said, leading Sam to a seat beside her on the couch Martin had been lying on an hour before, leaving the oversize armchair for Olivia and Martin to share.

Dropping the bag he'd emptied, Sam settled in beside Sylvia. Close beside her.

And Olivia sat forward. "I've seen you before," she said. "The morning I picked my mother up from the cruise…"

She glanced at Sylvia then. "You didn't go on that cruise with Gloria and Sandy."

Her mother shook her head.

"You lied to me?"

This was most definitely not turning out to be the lovely family Christmas memory she'd been envisioning. That her mother had gone on the cruise with a man fazed her not at all. That Sylvia hadn't been honest with her…

Hurt. Badly.

"Being a parent is tough," Sylvia said, her gaze clear and straightforward as she looked from Olivia to Martin. "There aren't always right choices. Clear choices. Easy ones. Some of them are just crap-shoots."

She'd lied. Seeing that that wasn't a good parental choice was easy. Trust was everything. Most partic-ularly between a parent and a child.

Between family members in general.

"My life with you has been filled with situations that had no good answers, Olivia," she said. "I gave you up out of a mother's love. It broke my heart. I went into a depression that would have killed me if my own mother hadn't held on to me. While she was holding on to you for me. But my giving you up gave you a stable home you could trust. And when I came back into your life, I paid again for that choice. Because you didn't trust me. For the past ten years, and for as long as I'm alive, I put you first. Period. It's you. No matter what."

She glanced at Sam.

"And I'm still learning what that means. Slowly. Because I didn't have your growing-up years to teach me. I'm like a new mom but I've got an adult kid."

Olivia's heart reached out to the woman. But she wouldn't let herself get past the lie. Somewhere there had to be lines drawn. Boundaries.

"I didn't tell you about Sam because I didn't want

you to think I was abandoning you for him. You've been so lost, sweetie. Decorated in your field, saving lives, strong enough to deal with the painful things you see every day—and lost, too. I'm your family. Your person. I wasn't going to have you thinking that I was moving on. Or to feel, in any way, like a third wheel."

Oh. God. No. Olivia felt as though her face had been in the sun too long. It tingled. Burned. And then chilled. The version of herself she was seeing, through her mother's words, and things Martin had said, too, was showing itself.

"In my selfish grief, I've robbed you of your life," Olivia said, her voice barely discernible. She turned to Martin. "And you, too."

The whole time she'd been shutting off her heart, being the best neonatologist she could possibly be, those who'd loved her had been carrying her.

She forgave her mother her lie. And Martin his need to move on apart from her. Hated what she'd become.

She'd been so afraid of loving, and losing…thinking she was tending to others, and she'd really only been tending to herself. Using her job to hide.

And her need for independence to shut out those who'd needed her.

That stopped in that instant.

"Thanksgiving…you were with Sam?" she asked.

Sylvia nodded.

"And this afternoon? Your plans are with him?"

Her mother nodded again. Olivia nodded, too, far too conscious of Martin sitting silently beside her. She could only imagine what he was thinking.

But wouldn't blame him if it had to do something with resenting her selfishness.

"So," she said, and turned to Sam, tried to give him a welcoming smile, "what are your intentions with my beautiful mother?"

He looked at Sylvia and she shook her head, standing up and heading out toward the kitchen, saying, "I'm going to get our mimosas, and then we should open presents."

About to disagree, to push for answers, Olivia met Sam's gaze and sat back.

It was time for her to learn how to be a good daughter. Most particularly if she ever hoped to be half the mother Sylvia was.

Chapter Twenty

While Martin was a bit perplexed by what was going on, he was surprised to realize that he had no desire to be anywhere else.

It was Christmas morning. Accusations were flying. Conversation was intense. A stranger had been dropped unexpectedly into their mix. Things were messy and, he figured by Sylvia's abrupt departure for alcohol-laced orange juice, about to get messier, and he wanted to be right where he was. Sitting next to Olivia.

When Sylvia returned with two champagne glasses, handing one to Sam, it was as though the past fifteen minutes hadn't happened. As though they were a family of four sitting down for a normal celebration.

She bent to the tree, pulling out packages. Handing them around. To Olivia. To Sam. Martin didn't care that there'd be nothing for him. He had money to buy anything that could be wrapped and put under a tree. And knew he'd been a last-minute addition.

When she handed him one, he stopped—and, for the first time since he'd awoken that morning, wished he wasn't there. He had nothing to give anyone.

You couldn't take if you didn't give. A rule his parents had ingrained in him since before he could remember having a thought of his own.

And then he saw the name on the tag. The gift was from Olivia. He opened it, laughing at the T-shirt with the front sporting a silk screen of a shirt and tie. She'd teased him forever about his inability to take a day off and wear a T-shirt. There was no doubt in his mind he'd wear that one.

Maybe just in his own condo. But he'd think of her every time he put it on.

There were other gifts from her, as well. A digital photo frame preloaded with photos of himself and his parents. She'd scanned all the photos when they were married. He'd never known what had happened to those scans. The originals were in a box in one of the closets at home.

He opened a shirt and tie combination, as well. His exact size. And from the designer he wore, in colors he preferred. And then there was the golf club. He'd coveted the putter once upon a time. Could never let himself spend that much money on a single club for playing a game. No matter how wealthy he'd become, there'd still be, inside of him, a part of the boy who'd grown up with his parents

He couldn't help getting up and taking a couple of small swings with it—and when he met her gaze as he did so, and saw the joy there, he almost kissed her. Probably would have, in spite of it being a colossal mistake at that point, if her mother and Sam hadn't been sitting right there, watching them.

As the packages dwindled, one by one, he was reminded of Christmas mornings with his parents, and how he hated to see the present opening come to an end. Not because he wanted more stuff, but because his parents had always been so happy during those hours. Their gifts hadn't been much. Stuff they all needed. Soap. Toilet paper, even. But each present was wrapped and opened with squeals and fun.

He hadn't had that kind of a real, bone-deep good time since his parents had died. Until right then.

With one package left under the tree, he sat back, sure, since it was in Sylvia's wrapping paper, that it was for Olivia, eager to watch her open whatever it was, figuring, since Sylvia had saved it for last, that it had to be good.

Sam picked up the package.

And brought it to Martin.

Confused, he glanced at Olivia, who looked about as confused as he was.

"Open it," Sylvia said, smiling at him, but with a hint of tears in her eyes.

He found a piece of tape. Slowly unhinged it. Feeling awkward. And a bit curious. The package wasn't all that big. Robe-box size. And wasn't heavy. Needing to be off the hot seat suddenly, he ripped into it. And unveiled…a robe box.

His ex-mother-in-law, who was more suited,

age-wise, to be his wife than her daughter was, had bought him a robe for Christmas? When she hadn't even known he was going to be there?

And left the gift to last?

Olivia was frowning, glancing from the box to her mother.

The box wasn't taped. He lifted the lid. And then the tissue paper.

And froze.

There, laying in a bed of white cloudlike material, were the onesies, T-shirts, sleepers and even a tiny cap that Olivia had given him the night she'd told him she was pregnant with Lily. The present had been how she'd broken the news to him. By having him open a different box, with different wrapping, bearing the very same gift. He didn't have to lift the pieces to know that every single one of them bore the same message.

I Love My Daddy.

For a second, as Olivia saw what lay in Martin's box, her heart soared. Muscle memory from long ago, and the hours she'd looked at those very same clothes, thinking her dreams were all coming true. That no woman could ever be happier.

That she'd found her home.

And then she looked away. Wondering how her mother could be so cruel. How she even…

"I saved them." Sylvia's voice, laced with emotion,

reached her ear. "I've kept them, all these years...
not knowing why...but knowing that they had to be
saved. They don't belong in my keeping anymore. I
don't know if they belong anywhere. I just know that
I had to give them back to you. And when Olivia told
me you were going to be here this morning... I had
Sam wrap them and bring them over."

Olivia couldn't look at the clothes. Or Martin.
Or her mother.

She met Sam's gaze. And it was kind. Filled with
an understanding she had to be imagining. And a
wisdom she desperately needed to access.

"I...can't believe... Thank you." Martin was
speaking. His voice was filled with something
sounding like awe.

She glanced at him. Saw the way he was looking
at those baby clothes, and found her gaze heading
straight back to Sam.

"You asked what my intentions are with your
mother," the older man said then, looking nowhere
but at her.

She nodded. Fought the tears that were threaten-
ing to fall all over their lovely celebration.

"I want to marry her, but I've got this situation,"
Sam started, and Olivia was suddenly focused only
on him. "I wasn't a great dad. In fact, I was lousy at
it. I was an undercover cop and too dedicated to the
job to come home and play with blocks. And when
my wife told me she'd fallen in love with another

man, an elementary school principal, I gave her the divorce she wanted and custody of my son, too. Only things didn't turn out as I'd expected. My son, while smart and good in school, ended up in a lot of trouble that traveled with him through college and into his adult life. He's currently serving twenty years to life in a prison in Texas. He was allowing an illegal prescription drug business to be run out of his insurance office and was present during a drug deal where two people were shot."

She didn't know what to say. Couldn't believe such a seemingly kind, soft-spoken man would be in such a situation. Knew there had to be a whole lot more to the story. One she figured she was going to hear at another time.

"You surely don't think that because you have a son in prison you can't marry my mom," she said.

And wasn't all that surprised when he shook his head.

"No, it's that I have to ask her to be a mother to my grandson, a fifteen-year-old kid who's heading down the same path as his father unless I can somehow find a way to change that course."

"You have custody of him?"

"Just got the final order yesterday. I'm supposed to pick him up from foster care this evening."

"What happened to his mother?" It didn't matter to the point at hand. She asked, anyway.

"She died in a car accident fourteen years ago.

My son was driving. And drunk. From what I understand, she was drunk, too. They were too young to start a family. Just eighteen. From what I'd heard, her death had straightened him out. I tried to reach out, but my son wanted nothing to do with me."

"While I'm fully supportive of Sam's need to take in his grandson, and wouldn't have it any other way," Sylvia said, "I was resistant to deepening our relationship as this boy is going to need a solid family. Hours of time every day and—"

"You're a certified counselor," Olivia said. "Who better than you to help him?"

"I wouldn't think about taking in another child and having my own feel as though I'm not putting her first, most particularly when I didn't raise my own."

It was like the clouds had opened above, deluging Olivia with insights, perspectives…and truths. Her mother loved her enough to give up her life a second time for her. Because that's what mothers did. No matter how many times it took.

And Sylvia had a strength far greater than any Olivia was showing. Her mother was willing to risk everything again and again, no matter the pain that might result.

Because that's what love did.

"Sylvia and I were talking last night," Sam said, including Olivia and Martin equally in his conversation, looking back and forth between the two of them. "About the fact that you've got a heartbeat now. And so much baggage between the two of you. We both feel as though we failed at being parents, in spite of the fact that our love for our children comes first in our hearts. And we both feel as though we're the last people who should be giving parental advice. But after you called this morning—" he looked at Olivia "—and told your mother that you and Martin weren't getting back together…"

She felt Martin stiffen beside her, but didn't dare look at him as their "baggage" was split right open there in the midst of Christmas morning wrapping paper.

"I told her that it seemed like we were being given second chances to be parents ourselves. And that's why I'm here."

He took a breath. No one else moved.

Sam looked at Martin first. "I'm old enough to be your father," he said. "And I'm taking in a fifteen-year-old boy who I've never met and who isn't particularly thrilled to be moving to Marie Cove. That boy is going to need a family, by the way, and from what Sylvia tells me, you know a lot about teenage kids and giving them incentives to keep them out of trouble."

"Give someone a fish he eats for a day, teach him to fish he feeds himself for life," Martin said, just as Olivia had heard him at a podium the one time she'd accompanied him to a Fishnet function. The familiar saying was something he'd learned from his parents, a theory by which they'd lived, and the basis of Fishnet.

"She told me about your nonprofit," Sam said. "And also about your struggle to see yourself as a father at forty-one. I'm suggesting that you find a way."

Oh God. Olivia wanted to be gone from the conversation. The chair. The room.

"I'm older now than you will be when your child is my grandson's age. And I've realized that it's not the age that matters. It's the love. The willingness to give it. And accept it. I'm his family. I'm all he's got. And the heartbeat you heard…you're that baby's father."

Silence fell as Sam sat forward, his elbows on his knees, looking at both of them again. Sylvia was watching him, not Olivia and Martin.

"I get that the two of you have suffered a loss I hope to God I never understand. I get that you know a pain I've never felt. But what I also know, with the wisdom life has given me, is that you've been given this second chance and you don't want to be sixty and looking back and seeing yourself not taking it.

"Life took from you, and now it's giving back. Are you really going to tell it 'no thank you'?"

This time when silence fell, it stayed there. Hanging around them all. Slowly encapsulating them. Olivia thought about breakfast. Expected Sylvia to spring up and announce that it was time to eat. Gloss over the tension.

"I told Sam this morning that I'll marry him,"

Sylvia said instead. "I'm watching you struggle to open yourself up to life again and doing nothing but helping you stay safe in your stagnant world. So, as of tomorrow, you're going to have a stepfather and stepbrother added to your family. Not officially yet, of course. We have to get a marriage license, but we're bringing Luke home with us and he's going to need a family." She looked at Martin. "And I hope he has you in his life, as well," she said. "He needs a role model."

Sam stood, pulled a mini flash drive case out of his pants pocket and handed it to Martin. "After I retired from the LAPD I took up music, of all things," he said. "I made this for you two last night. No matter what you decide to do, I'd ask that you listen to it, together."

Olivia wasn't sure Martin would even take the drive.

But she knew that she would take him. In any capacity. No matter what the future might hold.

She hadn't looked at him. But she took his hand next to her. Threaded her fingers in between his. He was still sitting there. And she was there for him.

No matter what he decided.

Still.

Sam's drive traveled in the front pocket of Martin's jeans for the rest of that day. As soon as he'd taken it, slid it in his pocket, Sylvia had jumped up and announced that they should all just take a breather, freshen up the mimosas none of them had finished and enjoy breakfast. Table conversation was, as though by order, lighthearted. Getting-to-know-you stuff and hearing how Sam and Sylvia had met when she'd been treating a cop buddy of his and he'd come to pick the guy up from a session. After breakfast and cleanup they'd had all the paper in the living room to clear out. Presents to stack. And for Sylvia and Sam to load up. They'd brought over their gifts for each other so that Sam would have something to open. And not long later it had been time for Martin and Olivia to head to the Applegates', where there was more holiday cheer, presents and everyone being happy.

Though they weren't scheduled to do so, they made a drive into Fishnet, as well, before heading back to Marie Cove. The teenagers had had a traditional Christmas morning with multiple presents under the tree for everyone; Fishnet sought to be the parental presence the kids didn't have. The older residents were treated the same, with presents just like any other college kid would have at home on break. What Fishnet couldn't fund, Martin did personally.

Because everyone deserved a chance.

Or a second one. He'd been thinking all day about what Sam had said. Was he going to tell his second chance, no thank you? Could he pretend even for a second that he wouldn't give his life to hold his child wearing a T-shirt that said "I Love My Daddy"?

Could he forget how many times he'd looked at the little sleeper Liv had given him, the cap, and pictured his little girl wearing it in her crib at night?

Yeah, he was struggling to see himself as a father at forty-one...because he knew the risk. And what kind of a man did that make him, that he'd let a child of his go fatherless because he was afraid of being hurt?

Sam had suggested he "find a way."

And Sylvia had announced that Olivia had told her that morning that she and Martin were through.

He'd pretty much come to that conclusion the night before, but to hear her mother say it, to know that it was a done deal before he'd accepted the reality...

Most of the way home, they talked about the day, the people, their impressions, funny moments. And as he exited the freeway at the Marie Cove exit, silence fell. The day was ending. Holiday cheer was done.

He pulled into the garage of her condo building and parked. She hadn't invited him in, or to spend the night. But all his stuff was still upstairs.

They went up together, without speaking. He didn't know what to say.

Martin had always been the guy who was good with words. The one who could always find the right thing to say. Something to say to make those he was with feel good.

Inside, he gathered up his things slowly. Stacked

the gifts by the door. Zipped up his overnight satchel and dropped it by the gifts.

Olivia sat on the couch with the tree lights on, her bootless feet curled up beneath her.

"Come, sit," she said when he'd taken as long as he could to get his stuff together and still wasn't ready to head out.

His time was up for good. He knew it. Knew what he had to do. Just had to find the guts to do it. Who knew the great Martin Wainwright, millionaire at twenty-two, eligible bachelor, was really a coward?

His hand brushed his thigh as he stepped slowly toward her and he felt the flash drive. Grabbing it like a man with a life raft, he said, "Wait. We should probably play this…"

And maybe, as they listened to Sam's music, words would come to him. No, he had the words. What he needed was the courage.

Did he dare hope that a sixty-year-old self-professed father failure would have the ability to make music that could inspire weak men to greatness?

Grabbing the remote, Olivia turned on the home theater while he inserted the drive and came to sit beside her on the couch. Right beside her.

There was no more room for pretense between them.

She hit Play and a soft, melodic riff filled the room. Some kind of electric piano, not digitized, synthesized music, but notes that flowed from one to the other, sounding like sadness and hope all at once. There was no percussion, nothing to keep rhythm, just what he was assuming was Sam's fingers on keys, until...there came a gurgle. And then another. In perfect rhythm.

"It's our heartbeat song," Olivia whispered, tears coming to her eyes.

Their heartbeat song.

It washed over him. Through him. Filling him.

Like a miracle from Santa Claus. Or a father's gift from Sam.

"Liv?"

"Yeah?"

"Will you marry me, again?"

He felt her stiffen as she jerked toward him, her gaze studying his fiercely. "You don't have to do this," she whispered.

He didn't break that look, didn't need to. Didn't want to.

"Oh, yes, I do," he said, his certainty strengthened by the power he was letting back into his life. "I'm done running. Done staying so busy I don't have time to grieve what's missing. All I ever wanted was a family. I was so happy as a kid. And then, when I lost my parents, one after the other, when I was in college, I just kept telling myself I had to hold on because I had my own family ahead of me. Like the one I had with them. The day I met you, I knew, I just knew I'd found that family. And then...when we lost Lily… I didn't know what to do. How to reach you in your grief. How to let you inside mine. And I lost you, too. Something died in me, and honestly, I was glad to have it gone."

He wasn't proud of himself. Was ashamed of what he'd become.

"Please, Liv, give us another chance. We've learned so much from our mistakes, let us gain from our own loss. We know to be emotionally honest with each other now. To turn to each other when we need comfort, rather than just trying to comfort the other or fix things. We need to be friends, partners, not just lovers… Please, help us learn to be those things."

Lifting the remote, she turned the recording back on again, and said, "I've already given us the second chance. And of course, I'll marry you again. It's always been you, Martin."

"It's always been you, Liv, for me, too. I can change the world on my own, but I can't find happiness without you."

"We have no guarantees that the baby's going to make it through gestation."

"Fear lives here, Liv. It's a fact of our lives. Because we know how badly life can hurt, and there are never guarantees that it won't hurt us again. But if we're fighting the fear together, a whole bunch of joy is going to live here, too." He was finally getting it. His home life growing up had been nearly idyllic for him, but it couldn't have been easy for his parents.

And yet, there'd been so much joy. Not just for him, but for them, too. He'd felt it emanating off them. Had fed from their happiness.

Just as he and Liv and whatever children they had in their lives fed off from theirs.

Getting up, he went to his bag. Pulled out the small black velvet case he'd brought with him and handed it to her.

"I saw this and had to buy it for you," he said. "Even when I was still running scared, I knew I had to find a way to open up to who we had to be."

She opened the case. A tear dripped down on the exquisite gold, catching color from the Christmas lights.

"You're the mother of our children, Liv. That's a given. But what this pendant reminded me was that, without me, you wouldn't be a mother. It reminds me that for every mother and child, there has to be a father, too. It's a sacred gift. And it's mine to accept, as long as I'm not a first-class idiot and throw it away. I've been an idiot long enough. I've run from the pain long enough. I don't know what the future looks like in terms of lifestyle—not yet, anyway. I just know that all the traveling in the world couldn't keep me from you. And I suspect the traveling was more of an excuse than a valid reason to stay away."

"I love you, Martin. So, so much."

"I love you, too. With my heart achingly wide open this time."

Taking the remote he put the recording on re-peat and took Liv into his arms. Kissing her with a brand-new passion, a deeper passion, born from the hope of forever.

The song played again.

And again.

Their Christmas heartbeat song.

Filling them with everything they needed to wel-come their future.

Epilogue

A deep, strained groan filled the air. Followed by two encouraging voices.

"Breathe. That's it, you've got this," they said one after the other, over the other, with the other.

And behind the litany, underneath it, surrounding it, filling the private, well-lit birthing room, with its couch and chairs and windows, were the soft sounds of an electric keyboard, and the gurgle-gurgle rhythm of Samantha Jane Wainwright's heartbeat, recorded at their first ultrasound seven months ago.

"We have a head," the doctor said. And, in the next second, held up a full, messy, breathing body.

"She's here," the woman beside the bed said, and then, frowning, moved to the doctor's side and, as she professionally and quickly cut the umbilical cord, moved her gaze over every inch of the body that was squirming and starting to fuss. "Quick, get her to the warmer," she said. "And weigh her…"

"She's fine, Dr. Wainwright," the doctor's voice said. "You know we've got this, piece of cake. And I think you need to see to your husband. Now, Beth…"

The doctor continued talking and tended to his business with his patient.

Beth responded to him when necessary, but mostly she was wearing a serene smile as she looked at the couple holding each other, crying, as they stood, cheeks pressed together, watching as, just inches away from them, the nurse tended to their newborn daughter.

"Okay, who wants to hold her first?" the nurse asked minutes later, turning with a bundled blanket that had the most perfectly angelic, robust baby face showing.

"We do," the couple said together, and, arms entwined on one side, reached with their others to support the baby between them.

With those simple words, and that gathering in of the tiny form, they became the family they'd always been meant to be.

* * * * *

COMING NEXT MONTH FROM

⒣ HARLEQUIN

SPECIAL EDITION

#2869 THE FATHER OF HER SONS
Wild Rose Sisters • by Christine Rimmer
Easton Wright now wants to be part of his sons' lives—with the woman he fell hard for during a weeklong fling. Payton Dahl doesn't want her sons to grow up fatherless like she did, but can she risk trusting Easton when she's been burned in the past?

#2870 A KISS AT THE MISTLETOE RODEO
Montana Mavericks: The Real Cowboys of Bronco Heights
by Kathy Douglass
During a rare hometown visit to Bronco for a holiday competition, rodeo superstar Geoff Burris is sidelined by an injury—and meets Stephanie Brandt. Geoff is captivated by the no-nonsense introvert. He'd never planned to put down roots, but when Stephanie is in his arms, all he can think about is forever...

#2871 TWELVE DATES OF CHRISTMAS
Sutter Creek, Montana • by Laurel Greer
When a local wilderness lodge almost cancels its Twelve Days of Christmas festival, Emma Halloran leaps at the chance to convince the owners of her vision for the business. But Luke Emerson has his own plans. As they work together, Luke and Emma are increasingly drawn to each other. Can these utter opposites unite over their shared passion this Christmas?

#2872 HIS BABY NO MATTER WHAT
Dawson Family Ranch • by Melissa Senate
Nothing will change how much Colt Dawson loves his baby boy. Not even the shocking news his deceased wife lied about Ryder's paternity. But confronting Ava Guthrie about his ex's sperm-donor scheme doesn't go as planned. Will Ava heal Colt's betrayed heart in time for a Wyoming family Christmas?

#2873 THE BEST MAN IN TEXAS
Forever, Texas • by Marie Ferrarella
Jason Eastwood and Adelyn Montenegro may have hit it off at a wedding, but neither of them is looking for love, not when they have careers and lives to establish. Still, as they work together to build the hospital that's meaningful to them both, the pull between them becomes hard to resist. Will they be able to put their preconceived ideas about relationships aside, or will she let the best man slip away?

#2874 THE COWBOY'S CHRISTMAS RETREAT
Top Dog Dude Ranch • by Catherine Mann
Riley Stewart has been jilted. He needs an understanding shoulder, so Riley invites his best friend, Lucy Snyder, and her son on his "honeymoon." But moonlit walks, romantic fires, the glow of Christmas lights—everything is conspiring against their "just friends" resolve. Will this fake honeymoon ignite the real spark Riley and Lucy have denied for so long?

**YOU CAN FIND MORE INFORMATION ON UPCOMING HARLEQUIN TITLES,
FREE EXCERPTS AND MORE AT HARLEQUIN.COM.**

HSECNM1021

SPECIAL EXCERPT FROM

⟨H⟩ HARLEQUIN
SPECIAL EDITION

*Nothing will change how much Colt Dawson loves his
baby boy. Not even the shocking news his deceased wife
lied about Ryder's paternity. But confronting
Ava Guthrie about his ex's sperm-donor scheme doesn't
go as planned. Will Ava heal Colt's betrayed heart in
time for a Wyoming family Christmas?*

Read on for a sneak peek at
His Baby No Matter What,
*the next book in the Dawson Family Ranch miniseries
by Melissa Senate!*

"I wasn't planning on getting one," Ava said. "I figured
it would be make me feel sad, celebrating all alone out at
the ranch. My parents gone too young. And this year, my
great-aunt gone before I even knew her. My best friend
after the worst argument I've ever had. I love Christmas,
but this is a weird one."

"Yeah, it is. And you're not alone. I'm here. Ryder's
here. And like you said, you love Christmas. That house
needs some serious cheering up. I want to get you a tree
as a gift from me to you for our good deal."

"It *is* a good deal," she said. "Okay. A tree. I have a
box of ornaments that I brought over in the move to the
ranch."

He pulled out his phone, did some googling and found a Christmas-tree farm that also sold wreaths just ten minutes from here. He held up the site. "Let's go after Ryder's nap. While he's asleep, we can have that meeting—I mean, *talk*—about our arrangement. Set the agenda. The… What would you call it in noncorporate speak?"

She laughed. "Maybe it is a little nice having a CEO around here," she said, then took a bite of her sandwich. "You get things done, Colt Dawson."

He reached over and touched her hand and she squeezed it. Again he was struck by how close he felt to her. But he had to remember he was leaving in two and a half weeks, going back to Bear Ridge, back to his life. There was a 5 percent chance, probably less, that he'd ever leave Godfrey and Dawson. But he'd have this break, this Christmas with his son, on this alpaca ranch.

With a woman who made him think of reaching for the stars, even if he wouldn't.

Don't miss
His Baby No Matter What *by Melissa Senate,*
available November 2021 wherever
Harlequin Special Edition books and ebooks are sold.

Harlequin.com

HSEEXP1021